DISCARD

You'll want to read these inspiring books by Lurlene McDaniel

Angels in Pink

Kathleen's Story
Raina's Story
Holly's Story

One Last Wish Novels

Mourning Song
A Time to Die
Mother, Help Me Live
Someone Dies, Someone Lives
Sixteen and Dying
Let Him Live
The Legacy: Making Wishes Come True
Please Don't Die
She Died Too Young
All the Days of Her Life
A Season for Goodbye
Reach for Tomorrow

Other Fiction

Briana's Gift
Letting Go of Lisa
The Time Capsule
Garden of Angels
A Rose for Melinda
Telling Christina Goodbye
How Do I Love Thee: Three Stories
To Live Again
Angel of Mercy • Angel of Hope
Starry, Starry Night: Three Holiday Stories
The Girl Death Left Behind
Angels Watching Over Me
Lifted Up by Angels
Until Angels Close My Eyes
I'll Be Seeing You
Saving Jessica
Don't Die, My Love
Too Young to Die
Goodbye Doesn't Mean Forever
Somewhere Between Life and Death
Time to Let Go
Now I Lay Me Down to Sleep
When Happily Ever After Ends
Baby Alicia Is Dying

From every ending comes a new beginning. . . .

Lurlene McDaniel

angels in pink

Holly's Story

*I would like to express my gratitude to Jan Hamilton Powell and Mickey
Milita of Erlanger Medical Center, Baroness campus, for their invaluable
help in shaping this series. And a special thank-you to Sergeant
Tim Carroll of the Chattanooga Police Department for his assistance.*

Published by Laurel-Leaf
an imprint of Random House Children's Books
a division of Random House, Inc.
New York

This is a work of fiction. Names, characters, places, and incidents either
are the product of the author's imagination or are used fictitiously.
Any resemblance to actual persons, living or dead, events,
or locales is entirely coincidental.

Originally published in hardcover in the United States by Delacorte Press,
New York, in 2005. This edition published by
arrangement with Delacorte Press.

Laurel-Leaf and colophon are registered trademarks of Random House, Inc.

www.randomhouse.com/teens

**Educators and librarians, for a variety of teaching tools,
visit us at www.randomhouse.com/teachers**

RL: 5.6
ISBN: 978-0-440-23867-6

April 2007

Printed in the United States of America

10 9 8 7 6

To all my loyal and wonderful readers who are always asking for more stories. Thank you!

Though one may be overpowered,
two can defend themselves.
A cord of three strands is not quickly broken.

Ecclesiastes 4:12, NIV

Angels in Pink Volunteers' Creed

I will pass through this life but once.
If there is any kindness I can show, any good that I
can do, any comfort that I can offer, let me do it
now, for one day I will be gone and what
will remain is the memory of what I did for others.

one

"Is THERE ANYTHING more fab than summer vacation?" Raina St. James's question sounded more like a declaration. "No classes, no homework, nothing to look forward to except weeks and weeks of sunshine."

Raina and her friends were spending the day at Carson Kiefer's house, lounging by the pool, under a clear blue sunny sky. Burgers sizzled inside the mammoth grill on the patio, and the aroma mingled with the scents of sunscreen and chlorine.

"I heard the school board wants to have year-round classes," Holly Harrison said. She was sitting on a towel at the side of the pool painting her toenails a flamboyant shade of hot pink.

"Forget it," Carson said. "We need a break." He took a running leap off the diving board and cut like a knife through the water. He swam the length of the pool underwater, coming up beside Kathleen McKensie's float.

She opened one eye. "If you splash me, I'll shoot you."

"Crabby."

"I've just covered myself with sunscreen and I don't want it washed off." She lifted her sunglasses to look at him treading water next to her. His brown eyes danced and droplets of water clung to his buttery tanned shoulders. "If I didn't burn to a crisp without it, I wouldn't mind," she said. "But *que sera, sera.*" She resettled the dark glasses on her nose and rested her head again on the cushioned pillow of the float.

He tossed his head and slung beads of water over her body. "Did I get you wet?"

She ignored him.

"Want me to lick the water off?"

Instantly, her face flushed bright red. "Go away."

He laughed. "Maybe you'd taste like coconut."

"Pervert." She wasn't even mildly annoyed. It felt so good to be back with him, to be a part of his life again, she would have tolerated any amount of his teasing. The weeks she'd spent apart from him the past winter after she'd hung up on him over a spat about Stephanie Marlow had seemed like an eternity.

"I'm, like, so disrespected," he announced. He put his elbows on the float, leaned over her and ran his cool, wet tongue across her mouth.

Shivers shot up her spine. "Scram!" she hissed.

He laughed, arched backward like a dolphin and dove under the water.

Raina watched, amused, from the circle of Hunter's arms. They were sitting on a lounge chair together, Raina in front, and Hunter was smoothing lotion on her back. The stroke of his fingers was lulling her into drowsiness. He bent forward and nibbled on her earlobe. "He's right about the coconut taste," he whispered.

"I'll buy you an Almond Joy," she mumbled.

"You taste better."

"I'm flattered." Waves of contentment washed over Raina, mimicking the water lapping against the colorful tiled sides of the pool. Hunter would be home for the entire summer and she'd be with him every minute possible, between his job at the fast-food restaurant and her volunteer work with the Pink Angels program at Tampa's Parker-Sloan Hospital. Every minute.

"What do you hear from Emma?" Hunter asked, leaning back in the chair and pulling Raina against him.

"I talked to Jon-Paul last night. Emma's finally home. She was asleep when I called." Raina closed her eyes, conjuring up the faces of her sister and her husband, a sister she had never known existed until February.

"But she's doing all right?"

"She is now." It had been touch and go as Emma's doctors fought to stave off infections that threatened her new bone marrow, but after a hundred and ten days, she had been sent home to complete her recovery and begin her married life, cancer free.

"And you?" Hunter touched her hip in the area where bone marrow had been extracted to save Emma's life.

"You asked me the same thing yesterday. The answer's the same today. I'm fine. Just a small scar."

"Can I see?" He nuzzled her neck.

"I'm shocked you would ask. I mean with all these people looking on."

He laughed. One thing she could trust about Hunter was that he wouldn't look even if she stripped on the spot. "I'm not a prude."

"Yes you are." She twisted around and kissed him lightly. "That's what makes it work between us. I keep trying to jump your bones and you keep pushing me away."

"This will change when we get married."

Her heart did its usual stutter step. They talked about sex and marriage, but truthfully, huge hurdles lay in front of them. For starters, Hunter wanted to be a minister and had taken early admission to a small Christian college in Indiana the previous winter. She wasn't sure she even believed in God. Only Holly, Hunter's sister, realized the depth of their dilemma. Raina was worried about their having a future when they were such polar opposites in this area. Yet whenever she was with him, all she thought about was how much she loved him and about being with him forever.

"What if I get a better offer?" she asked playfully.

"Then I'll just have to take the guy out."

"That sounds pretty hostile—for a minister."

"Think of Samson. Hey, I'm tough. I'm the guy who got into a fistfight over you, remember?"

How could she forget? Tony Stoddard's bad mouth had almost destroyed her relationship with Hunter. "Don't joke about that, Hunter," she said quietly. "I don't think I'll ever be able to joke about it."

His arms tightened around her. "I was the idiot, not you."

She knew he wanted to make it up to her for the way he'd treated her after Tony's "revelation," but he didn't need to. She loved him and wanted to be with him forever—yet the hurdles remained.

Carson hoisted himself out of the pool. "I'd better turn the burgers." He padded over to the grill, raised the lid and stared down. "Um—I think they're burned."

Holly went over and confirmed his suspicion. "Hopelessly burned."

"Dad's never burn."

"He stands over them full-time," Kathleen called. She had straddled the float and paddled to the shallow end of the water, where she used the steps to exit the pool. She walked over to the grill.

The three of them stared in dismay at the charred remains of their lunch.

"Too bad. I'm starved," Kathleen said.

Carson turned off the grill. "So how does everybody feel about pizza?" The agreement was unanimous, so he picked up his cell phone and hit a single button.

Incredulous, Kathleen asked, "You have the pizza parlor on speed dial?"

Carson grinned. "A guy's got to eat." He slipped his arm around her.

Holly hung back, feeling as left out as she always did. She'd turned sixteen in May and now had her driver's license, not that it did her a whole lot of good. Her parents only allowed her to drive Hunter's beat-up car solo and only if and when he wasn't using it, which wasn't often. Her emancipation wouldn't go into full effect until he returned to college in September—if then. But it wasn't the car issue that bothered her the most. It was the lack of a boyfriend, a guy of her own, a boy who took her out on dates or came with her when she hung out with Raina and Hunter, Kathleen and Carson.

In mid-May, the e-mails from Shy Boy had stopped as suddenly and mysteriously as they had begun. Her e-mails to him bounced back to her mailbox, so she was no closer to knowing who he was than when he'd first contacted her in February. She'd printed out all their communications and kept them in a notebook stuffed between her mattress and box spring, because, of course, her parents knew nothing about Shy Boy. They would never have approved, so she'd printed and then deleted the messages as soon as they'd arrived. She'd read them so many times that she could quote them.

HOLLY: Are you some 35-year-old pervert, pretending to be sixteen?

SHY BOY: I'm seventeen, and not a pervert . . . well, I'm not most of the time.

HOLLY: Why don't you want to meet me face to face?

SHY BOY: I know what your face looks like. It's the face of an angel.

HOLLY: But I don't know what YOU look like!

SHY BOY: My mother thinks I'm handsome.

HOLLY: I should believe her because . . . ?

SHY BOY: Because mothers don't lie. And because it's what's inside a person that counts, not what's on the outside.

HOLLY: So . . . are you saying that you
have a face only a mother can love?
SHY BOY: My face is decent. Honest. And
I only have eyes for YOU.

Then the e-mails had stopped. She felt irritated and impatient with him. And she felt sorry for herself. She finally had a boy interested in her, and he was like a phantom. She couldn't see him or touch him. Raina had said, "Savor the moments. If he got hold of you once, he'll do it again."

And Kathleen had said, "Remember how long it took me to get it together with Carson. Be patient."

Easy for them to say. They had their guys locked in their arms and their hearts. The only bright spot in Holly's life this summer was the Pink Angels program. Volunteering at the hospital was what got her out of bed these bright summer mornings. That and the remote possibility that one day soon, she'd turn on her computer and Shy Boy would have sent her another e-mail, this time setting up a time and place for them to meet.

two

KATHLEEN SNUGGLED AGAINST Carson in his media room as the DVD movie credits rolled. Their friends had just left and they were alone. She felt relaxed, sleepy. He kissed her forehead. "You awake?"

"Maybe. Who's asking?"

He laughed deep in his throat. "You could spend the night. My folks are away."

She woke immediately. "My mother isn't away. She'd be frantic if I didn't come home." She eyed him. "You're just giving me a hard time, aren't you?"

"Partly. I really would like to spend the night with you."

She swallowed hard and pushed away. "I'm not ready for that." Her nerves had grown as tight as bowstrings.

Carson caught her chin and stared into her eyes, his expression serious. "I know you're not. When you are, can I be first in line?"

"I'm amazed that you think there'd be a line."

A grin sneaked up one side of his mouth. "You underestimate your sex appeal. But you always have."

She felt color creeping up her cheeks. "If there's one thing I wish I could control, it's this blushing I do all the time," she grumbled.

He kissed her. "I think it's sexy."

"You're sweet to say so."

"*Sweet!* Don't let it get out. It'll ruin my reputation." He leaned back, resting his arms across the tops of the theater seats, in no hurry to take her home.

Kathleen relaxed. She didn't want to leave yet either. "What will you do all summer?" she asked. "Work at the hospital? Work in your dad and mom's office?" She'd met him the summer before when they'd both signed on to be Pink Angels volunteers, a job he had not taken seriously. His parents had made him come to their medical offices to work when he kept skipping out of the volunteer service.

"You really want to know?"

"Sure."

He stood and pulled her to her feet. "Come with me." He led her through a side door, almost hidden in the wall, into his bedroom suite. The suite consisted of two rooms, one filled with audio gear, a jukebox, a sofa and beanbag chairs, two desks and a computer. A pinball machine had been added since the last time she'd been there. A large bedroom and bath adjoined. Entire families lived in less space. "Look at this." He crossed to a desk and handed her a catalog from one of Tampa's technical colleges, folded back to a list of summer courses. He had circled "Introduction to Emergency Medical Training" and its description.

She read the paragraph quickly and looked at him. "You want to become an EMT? I thought you hated the idea of going into medicine."

"I hate the idea of practicing the kind of medicine that my parents and my brother and sister practice. That's years of study and internship and residency. No way. But this—I mean, it's so much more interesting. Going on 911 emergency calls in ambulances—that appeals to me. I'm not stuck in some hospital or office. I get to be outside. I get to really help people in the trenches."

His eyes shone as he talked, which surprised her. Carson had never been enthusiastic about anything that resembled work. He liked to party and drive fast, and he had numerous speeding tickets and groundings by his father to prove it.

"I think that's admirable." She chose her words carefully. "How long have you been thinking about this?"

"Longer than you would guess." He took the

booklet and put it back on his desk. "Ever since that night we found your mother passed out on the floor."

Kathleen would never forget that night and the sheer terror she'd felt at seeing her mother unconscious and not breathing. "You saved her life."

"I can't tell you what it felt like for me. She was in real trouble. A few minutes later and we'd have lost her. But when I blew air into her lungs and did chest compressions and she suddenly began to breathe again, well, I—I felt like a miracle worker." His voice had grown soft, his tone awed. He stared down at his hands. "I know that's how my dad feels. He opens a person's chest and sees a diseased heart and he fixes it. Unless he does, the person is going to die. Mom does the same thing with children and even babies. I finally get it. Doctors heal. I want to do that too, but not in the same way as them."

She was touched by the sincerity in his voice. "So this course you want to take, what do your parents think?"

"I haven't told them exactly. I just said I was going to do some extra study at the community college. That shocked them enough."

"But why haven't you said anything? They'd be pleased."

"Dad wants me to go to college. He'd never understand my wanting to be a lowly EMT."

"And you don't want to go to college?" She

couldn't imagine that. She'd wanted to go all her life. Education was a way into a good job and better money.

"I hate studying," he confessed. "I hate being cooped up in a classroom. If I went to college, I'd party and never go to classes. I'd be on probation before the end of the first grading period."

"You sell yourself short. Look how you've brought your grades up this past year."

"It was sheer torture. I'm telling you, college would be a waste of my time and Dad's money. I want to drop all my college prep courses in my senior year."

"Your dad—"

"Will have a seizure." Carson finished her sentence. "I can't help it. That's why I want to take this intro course this summer. If I do well, maybe it'll help Dad take off his blinders and see me as I really am."

Kathleen was seeing a side of Carson she'd not met before, a serious side that suffered from conflicts imposed by his overachieving and perfectionist family—good, kind people, but people who pressured him to be like them. He *was* different. His crazy antics were his way of telling it to the world. "Well, I think you should go for it," she said. "You'd make a wonderful EMT."

"You think so?"

She smiled. "Want a letter of recommendation from me and my mom?"

"I'll settle for a kiss." His familiar impish grin lit up his face.

"You want to kiss my mother?" She feigned shock.

"Just her daughter." He grabbed for Kathleen.

She ducked and skittered away into his bedroom, where he caught up with her and began to tickle her mercilessly. They fell into a laughing heap across his bed. They eventually grew quiet, gazing into each other's eyes. The sound of their breathing stirred the air.

"Dangerous place to be with me," he finally said.

"That goes both ways," she said, emboldened by a rush of adrenaline. She'd already been in his bedroom, but he didn't know it. She'd sneaked in once the summer before when he'd been upstairs, so she already knew what it looked like. It had an Asian motif done in chocolate brown, green and black, a carpet the color of grass and accents of bright red.

He stole his kiss, then sat upright, pulling her with him. "What do you think of the place?"

Her gaze swept the room and she hoped she looked as if it were the first time she'd seen it. "Not bad. You decorate it yourself?"

"Get real. But I did get to tell the decorator what I liked."

"You have good taste." She couldn't help

looking at the shelf of photos along one wall for the one of Stephanie she'd seen before. It had been moved, but it was still there. Boldly, she went over and picked it up. Aloud she read, " 'I won't forget our special summer. With much love, Steffie.' How charming."

He took it from her hands and slid it into a drawer. "I see the place so much, I don't notice such details. And I might add, I don't have a photo of you to replace it."

"I'll get right on it."

Stephanie Marlow was a sore point between them that had almost wrecked their romance at Christmastime. Stephanie hated Kathleen, and she held some mysterious power over Carson that led him to refuse to abandon his friendship with the girl.

"You are—um—over things with her, aren't you?" Carson asked.

"Well, you said she'll be away all summer, so I'll adjust to her absence." Kathleen tried to be flip, but still Carson's gaze looked guarded. "Plus you've convinced me that I'm the one for you," she added with a smile.

"She's been hired to do modeling shoots in the Islands and in London. Then she's off to Brazil to visit her mother, who'll probably never return to the States."

It rankled Kathleen that he knew Stephanie's schedule, but she didn't say so because it would only make Carson mad. "And I guess her father won't miss either of them?"

"He never has in the past."

Poor little Steffie, Kathleen thought sarcastically. She wished she'd stay in Brazil and forget her senior year at Bryce Academy with Carson. But of course she wouldn't. "With your taking that EMT course, you'll be busy too." She changed the subject.

"What about you? You headed into the Pink Angels again?"

Kathleen took a deep breath. "I'm thinking about getting a job. I almost got one last summer, but Raina insisted we all sign up to be Pink Angels—which I'm glad I did, but if I want new clothes for my senior year, I need to earn some money."

"I thought your mother got a job."

"Just part-time." Since her open-heart surgery, Mary Ellen's life had blossomed. She attended a multiple sclerosis support group and all their get-togethers, was even dating a member of the group and was working three days a week as a bookkeeper for a trucking firm. There were times when Kathleen wondered if Mary Ellen even thought about Kathleen's deceased father anymore. If she did, she didn't talk about him the way she used to. Kathleen added, "Besides, Mom shouldn't have to pay for all the things I want. I don't mind working. But don't say anything to

Raina and Holly. I haven't told them yet. We're supposed to report to Sierra on Monday for orientation." Sierra Benson was in charge of the program.

"How about in the fall? I thought you were counting on the credits you get for being in the program."

"That's what I want to talk to Sierra about. I want to go back in the fall for class credit, and I hope that not being involved this summer won't bump me from the program."

He shook his head and looked amused. "All for new clothes?"

How could he understand? He wanted for nothing material, while she wanted many things. Money was tight at her house. She didn't want to put pressure on her mother. "*Pretty* new clothes," she told him. "I can't go naked." A wicked grin crossed his face and she turned beet red. "Don't say a thing."

"What? You can't fault a guy for mental images, can you?"

"Erase them. And then take me home before I break curfew and get into trouble."

"I can get you into trouble without us leaving." He kissed her neck.

"I thought we agreed we should stay out of *that* kind of trouble."

He grinned. "For the time being. But not forever."

She blinked as he turned and exited the bedroom. Her heartbeat quickened and her mouth went dry as her insecurities resurfaced. Until Carson had come along, she'd never been seriously kissed. She had no doubt that he'd experienced much more, was probably used to getting anything he wanted from the girls he dated. Sophisticated girls. Girls like Stephanie Marlow. Kathleen was scared. She didn't want to lose Carson, but she didn't want to get in over her head either. She kept remembering what had happened to Raina. Carson wasn't vindictive and hateful like Tony, but what if he got bored with her? And with Stephanie waiting in the wings, he wouldn't be without love and affection for long. Of that, Kathleen was very sure.

three

"HELLO, KATHLEEN. READY to start another summer?" Sierra said, smiling up at Kathleen when she entered her office. "I'm making out the work schedule now, and even with the new recruits there's still plenty to do. I'm glad I have you veterans to fall back on. And don't worry, I won't put you anyplace with sick patients. Did you like your stint in the medical library? The director sure had glowing words about you."

Kathleen nervously licked her lips. This wasn't going to be easy. "I need to tell you something." Color crept up her neck and across her face as she explained her problem. She finished with "I love the program, and I'd like to come back for credit in the fall, but I—I really need a job this summer."

Sierra sat back and steepled her fingers. "I understand. I had to work all through college. It was tough, but I did it. Any prospects?"

"I'm filling out applications at department stores and also at a couple of restaurants for lunch shifts. There's a pharmacy not far from my house. Maybe they can use my help."

"Why leave? The hospital has plenty of paying jobs, and so long as we keep your hours within federal guidelines, your age shouldn't be a problem. Let me check into it."

Kathleen's heart leaped. "Will you?"

"Just hold off on taking a job until you hear from me, all right? I promise to get back to you quickly."

"I sure will. And thank you so much."

"I wouldn't want a little thing like money to get in the way of your medical career."

"But I—" Kathleen saw that Sierra was teasing, because everyone knew that Kathleen couldn't stand the sight of blood. Her blush deepened. "I'll wait to hear from you."

Sierra laughed and shooed her out of the office.

Holly hustled around the pediatric floor doing the chores Mrs. Graham had given her. So far she'd removed breakfast trays and delivered two get-well balloon baskets and six get-well cards to various kids in the rooms. This area was much more cheerful to work in than the pediatric oncology wing, but even though the kids there were much sicker, she liked working that area better. The kids tugged on her heartstrings. Some of them suffered so nobly. Many screamed their heads off whenever a doctor approached their beds, because they associated anyone in a white coat with pain, but they all seemed to like Holly. She played endless games of Go Fish and Yahtzee with them when they felt up to it.

One of the floor nurses called out, "Holly, there's a flower delivery downstairs in the gift shop for someone in the teen wing. Could you run down and get it and bring it up to the correct room? They missed it this morning, and the girl's having surgery this afternoon."

Holly took the elevator down. Except for her initial tour of the hospital when she'd first become a Pink Angel, she hadn't been in the teen wing the whole year that she'd volunteered. Down on the main floor, she went into the gift shop, where undelivered gifts were placed, and was surprised to see Kathleen behind the counter. "Is *this* your assignment?" Holly asked.

Kathleen looked sheepish and glanced at an older woman, clearly the one in charge, and asked, "Can I have a few minutes with my friend?"

The woman agreed, and Kathleen took Holly outside into the bustling atrium, where Holly said, "I can't be gone long. I'm supposed to be picking up a flower delivery. What's up?"

"When I got here, Sierra sent me down. I had asked for a real job. You know . . . the kind that pays money. Actually, I was going to quit the program because I really have to work this summer, but Sierra said she'd try and hook me up here."

"Why didn't you say something to me and Raina?"

"I was going to."

"When?" Holly sounded hurt.

"I didn't want Raina to go into lecture mode until I had my plan in place. You know how touchy she's been ever since she found out about Emma."

"Yes, but she's doing so much better since Hunter's been home."

"I let her talk me out of getting a job last summer because she wanted us all to be volunteers together, and I couldn't let her do it again. I really need the money."

"Good thing you caved last summer. You'd have never met Carson."

"True, but I can't face the medical floors like you and Raina do. A job in the gift shop is perfect for me. The best of both worlds this summer. I was planning to tell you all when we went home today. Mom baked me a cake and is having a little party to celebrate my minimum wage coup. Corny, huh? But she knows I wanted to be with my friends *and* make money."

Holly grinned. "Actually, I'm jealous because I didn't think to do the same thing."

Kathleen returned her smile and they walked back to the gift shop, where Kathleen introduced Holly to her supervisor and the main employee of the shop, Mrs. Nesbaum. "It's so good to have hired help again," the portly woman said. "The last girl just up and left without a word. Just didn't show up one day. You're not going to do that to me, are you?"

Kathleen assured her that she wouldn't, then walked Holly to the refrigerated unit that held an array of floral baskets. She found the one that Holly had been sent to retrieve and deliver. "See you in the parking garage at five," Kathleen said. "I'll tell Raina ASAP."

Holly set off to make her delivery. Her first impression of the teen floor was that it didn't look very cheerful. Pediatrics was bright and colorful, with murals and a kid-friendly playroom that was well stocked with toys, games and books. The teen floor looked like any of the hospital's adult floors—dull and uninteresting. Most of the doors were closed, meaning visitors should knock before entering. She wondered how many teens were on the floor, and what was wrong with them. Of course, hospital policy prohibited her from asking a patient such personal information. It could only be volunteered or surmised.

She found the room number of her delivery and knocked gently. No one answered, so she cracked the door and saw a girl asleep on a bed. Holly entered and placed the basket on the bedside table, hoping it would be the first thing she saw when she woke. The sleeping girl looked to be about thirteen, and a "nothing by mouth" order had been taped to the wall above her bed. Made sense, since she was going into surgery. Holly felt sorry for her and gave an involuntary shudder. The girl was too close to Holly's age for Holly to feel comfortable. She thought about asking her father, the fount of all theological knowledge, why kids got sick in the first place. Holly believed in God with all her heart, but the way he ran things didn't always make sense to her. Her father, Mike, often fell back on "Does the clay question the potter?"—an answer that annoyed her and solved nothing.

Holly heard a gurney coming down the hall and backed away from the sleeping girl. "I'll say a prayer for you," she whispered. She fled the teen wing, grateful to be away from the depressing place that housed people her own age wrestling with disease and pain—and ever so grateful that she wasn't one of them.

"You missed dinner," Raina's mother said as soon as she walked in the door that night.

"Kathleen's mother had a little party for her to celebrate Kathleen's new job in the hospital gift shop. No more volunteering for her this summer . . . steady work and steady pay," Raina answered stiffly.

"Good for Kathleen. You could have called me," Vicki said.

"Sorry," Raina said, without conviction.

"Are you going to be angry at me for the rest of your life?" Vicki crossed her arms.

"I'm not sure. Do you have any more secrets you 'forgot' to tell me?" Raina was talking about Emma, of course, the baby whom Vicki had given up for adoption years before Raina was born.

"Don't be hateful. I was trying to get on with my life."

"And if my sister hadn't gotten sick and needed bone marrow, and if I hadn't put myself in the national registry on a whim, would I have ever known about her?"

"I would have told you eventually."

"And will you tell *her* about our having the same father? She should know that."

"Maybe someday. She's struggling with so much right now."

Exasperated by Vicki's excuses, Raina fired at her, "You're playing God, Mother. She has a right to know."

"She has terrific adoptive parents who love her and who never expected me to walk back into her life. Plus her biological father is dead, so why muddy the water? What purpose would it serve except to make *you* feel better, or whatever it is you're feeling toward her? She's not a part of our lives, Raina."

"She's part of my life!" Raina cried. "I saved her life. Just because you don't want anything to do with her—"

"Stop it!" Vicki glared at Raina. "How dare you assume what I want? Do you think it's easy to give up a baby? Do you think I haven't thought about Emma every day since I gave her up? But I had *you* to think of and to raise, and a career to plan so that I could make a life for us. Because it's about us, you and me, and what's best for *us*."

"How nice to know I was the perfect substitute for the baby you really wanted."

Vicki's hand shot out at Raina's mouth so quickly that Raina never saw it coming, but she felt the sharp sting—it made her eyes water. For a stunned moment, neither one of them spoke. Raina's head was reeling. In spite of all the yelling matches they'd had over the years, she couldn't remember her mother's ever striking her. She watched Vicki's eyes fill with tears. "That hurt," Vicki whispered.

Raina couldn't answer. Shock mingled with fury. Her mother had slapped her. *Slapped* her.

Vicki backed away. "I've made so many sacrifices. And for what? For a daughter who doesn't think about my existence. And for another who hates me." She turned, her back ramrod straight, and ascended the stairs.

Raina watched her mother leave without apology, without concern for having slapped her. Raina seethed, but held herself in steely control. She would be eighteen in November. She would graduate next May. She could hang with Hunter all next summer, maybe go to college in the same area. Maybe she would forget college and get a job near Hunter. Anyplace would be better than here with her mother, who had once been like a best friend but who now seemed like her worst enemy.

four

As THE JULY Fourth weekend approached, Holly
realized that her summer was going to be a good
one. She hadn't had any major blowups with her
parents. She was well liked and trusted at the
hospital, and had been put in charge of the an-
nual ice cream social for the pediatric floor. She
was learning to sew and with her mother's help
had created a few fashionable (and acceptable)
outfits for back to school. And Shy Boy was
e-mailing her once again.

His first note read:

> Hello, pretty Holly. Sorry about my long
> silence, just know that it was good for me
> in one way, bad in another because I
> couldn't see you.

While his message was typically cryptic, he'd
inadvertently given her a big clue: wherever he
was, he was "seeing" her. She answered with a
chatty message about her summer so far, and

didn't bother to suggest meeting. Why humiliate herself? If he wanted to meet her, he'd ask. In the meantime, she let her imagination run, conjuring up exciting scenarios. He was a prince, closely guarded by security forces. He was a great athlete busy training for a marathon, or maybe the Olympics.

Yet for all the secrecy between them, she also liked him. He had substance and depth, features she had begun to appreciate over time. When they got into weighty matters, he often had something to say that she found thought-provoking. When she'd pointedly written, "Do you believe in God?" he had answered, "Of course I do. People need something to believe in besides fate. Or happenstance. Plus I'd hate to think that the here and now is all we have. Too much pain and suffering to make me want to believe that!"

"Earth to Holly."

Hunter's voice from behind made her jump.

She spun away from her computer screen. "Don't sneak up on me. You're supposed to knock before coming into my room."

"I did knock, but you were off in outer space. What are you doing, anyway?" He peered over her shoulder.

"Nothing." She quickly hit the Escape key. Better to lose her latest reply to Shy Boy than have Hunter see it.

His eyes narrowed. "You can't fool me, sis. You're somewhere you're not supposed to be, huh?"

"With parental controls in place? You must be joking."

"Your eyes go all shifty when you lie. Don't you know that's how Dad always catches you?"

She reddened. "Take a hike."

He laughed. "First we need to talk. Raina asked me to talk to my boss about donating free candy and balloons for that ice cream social. She said I should check it out with you, if it's something you want me to do."

"Anything you can get for free would be great. Do you think he'll do it?"

"Probably. He's a pretty nice guy. How much of each would you need?"

"I'll check with Sierra." Holly paused thoughtfully. "Actually, I'm thinking about expanding the event for next year."

"Expanding? Like how?"

"Like having a full-blown carnival on the grounds, and asking local businesses to donate prizes. I'd love to have a carousel, a few tame rides, some clowns, a petting zoo—stuff like that for the kids. We can get the community involved, raise some money for the hospital, and the sick kids will have a good time. The ice cream social is okay, but kind of rinky-dink. With a carnival, everybody wins. What do you think?"

"I think it sounds like a lot of work."

"The Pink Angels program can sponsor it and do a lot of the work."

"You and Raina are the most enthusiastic two people I know. Others may not be so committed."

"Then they'll just have to get committed, won't they?"

He cleared his throat, looking embarrassed. "Raina also wants me to dress up like a clown and pass out any stuff my boss might donate."

Holly grinned. "That's a great idea! If it works, we'll have you do it again next year."

"I'm going to feel stupid."

"It's for charity. And for the kids. They love that kind of stuff. Please do it."

Hunter shrugged. "I don't even know how to do clown makeup."

"Leave it to me. I'll make you look very clownish."

"That's what I'm afraid of."

"I'm so glad you're in love with Raina," Holly said with a laugh. "She knows just how to pull your strings."

Sierra was intrigued by Holly and Raina's suggestion for a carnival. "There are organizations that specialize in events like this. They set up fundraising for schools and churches. It would probably take about a year to get such an event arranged. Maybe we could do it in conjunction with the hospital's seventy-fifth anniversary! That's coming up next year. It would be a great fund-raiser if we invite the whole community. Let me check into it."

Raina and Holly exchanged smiles.

"Now, how about this year?" Sierra asked. "How's it coming along?"

After they gave her their report and the list of volunteers who'd signed up, they headed off to their separate floors and daily duties. Holly was just getting off the elevator when she saw a little boy coming down the hall, walking beside a woman pushing a baby in a stroller. She called out, "Ben? Is that you?"

The boy looked up and saw her and his face broke into a grin. He began running. Holly knelt and caught him when he threw himself into her arms, shouting, "Holly!"

She laughed and tousled his blond hair. "You look so grown-up." He must be close to seven now, she calculated. The last time she'd seen him, he'd been five and just completing his second round of cancer treatments.

He grinned and she saw that his two front teeth were missing, with one new tooth partially grown in. "I told Mom you'd be here."

The woman with the stroller came hurrying up. "Holly? I can't believe it! All he's talked about was seeing you again. I told him you probably wouldn't be here, but he was so sure. And he was right!"

Holly stood, and with her hand on Ben's shoulder, she gave Beth-Ann Keller an impromptu hug. "Is this your new baby?"

Beth-Ann beamed a smile down at the child in the stroller. "This is Howie. He was born last August, just after Ben came home." The plump-cheeked baby was happily chasing cheese crackers around the tray of his stroller.

"He's so cute."

"Cute as me?" Ben asked.

She squeezed him more tightly. "No one's as cute as you. You still my special boyfriend? Or did you go and fall in love with some first-grade girl?"

Ben made a face. "Girls have cooties."

"I'm a girl."

"You're different."

Because of his mother's difficult pregnancy, Holly had been Ben's best friend during his chemo treatments. She'd gone with him to every treatment, taking him for ice cream in the hospital cafeteria afterward, a ritual he'd loved despite frequently throwing up every bite once they returned to his room. Her heart seized as a thought struck her. "Why are you here?"

"Just a checkup," Beth-Ann said, as if sensing Holly's fear. "He's had some blood work done."

Ben held out his arm. A bright blue Band-Aid with drawings of Spider-Man stretched across the inside of his elbow. "I didn't even cry."

Holly's heart melted. "You're so grown-up."

Baby Howie gurgled. Beth-Ann said, "We should be going. It's a long drive home."

"I'm really glad I got to see you," Holly said. She hugged Ben goodbye.

"Am I *really* still your boyfriend?"

"You are," Holly said, making him grin more widely. She watched the elevator doors close and turned away, pressure in her chest and good feelings swimming through her. She thought of Shy Boy, then mumbled, "Yes, Ben. You're still my one and only. But I'll bet you'll leave me for a second grader. Oh yes. Bet you will."

"What's wrong?" Kathleen had gone over to Carson's after work, only to find him angry and agitated.

"Dad and I had a blowup." He paced his room, dodging the pinball machine and jukebox.

"About . . . ?" She knew he had a knack for getting into trouble, but so far this summer he seemed to be doing better.

"He found out I was taking the EMT course."

"What's so horrible about that? I would have thought he'd be glad."

Carson gave a derisive laugh. "It's not *real*

medicine. I told you he'd react badly. That's why I didn't tell him in the first place."

"But you like the course and you told me you've done well."

"I have. But Dad considers it beneath the House of Kiefer. He wants me to study traditional medicine. Become one of the Kiefer dynasty."

There had to be more going on. *Wait for it*, Kathleen told herself.

"Plus I told him I was dropping my college prep schedule for senior year. I mean, why should I suffer through trig and Latin if I'm going to be an EMT?"

"Maybe he's not steamed about your becoming an EMT so much as he is about your changing your schedule."

He whipped around. "Whose side are you on, anyway?"

"I'm not taking sides. I'm just trying to help. You know, he might be right about your changing your curriculum in your last year of high school. You've come so far and you're almost there."

"That stuff's hard." Carson slumped into a beanbag. "I'm not smart like my brother and sister. I have to study really hard and that's just for Cs."

"We all have to study hard." She dragged another beanbag across from his and flopped down. "Except for Holly. She skipped a grade way back when and she still doesn't break a sweat over the books."

"Well, I do," Carson said. "Busting my brain isn't how I want to spend my senior year. But more than that, I don't want to go to college—at least not for four years. I'm telling you, I can go two years to Tampa Tech and come out with an associate degree and take the EMT test. Becoming an EMT is what I want to do."

"Maybe he'll come around if you do well in school this year."

Carson scoffed. "He'll think he won if I back down."

She felt sympathetic, but wasn't sure how to console him. "Did you tell him how you felt after you saved my mother?"

"And she wasn't the only one I saved either," Carson blurted out.

"She wasn't? Who else?"

His face colored and Kathleen realized that it was something he hadn't meant to say. She held her breath, waited. He sat still, staring over her head, his jaw clenched.

"Tell me. Please."

"Steffie's." His eyes bored into hers. "I saved Stephanie's life when we were fourteen."

five

"WHAT ARE YOU talking about?" Kathleen's heartbeat had accelerated the moment he had said Stephanie's name. Hadn't she always felt there was some mysterious and perplexing element that linked Stephanie and Carson?

Carson's expression went dark as a thundercloud. "No one else knows."

She sat very still, hoping he would finally tell her what had happened.

"If anyone knew, we both could be in serious trouble."

"But it had to have happened when you were in like . . . ninth grade. Isn't there a statute of limitations?"

"She could have died."

Kathleen's heart constricted. "You don't have to tell me if you don't want to, Carson, but if you do, I'll always keep your secret, just like I kept Raina's secret about Tony all those years."

He laced his fingers behind his head and hunkered down in the squishy chair. "If I tell you,

you can't ever tell anyone, not even Raina or Holly."

Kathleen nodded.

"You already know how Steffie has grown up with absentee parents. Nothing but a few housekeepers along the way."

And all the money in the world, Kathleen thought, without much sympathy.

"My mother felt sorry for her and sort of took Steffie under her wing. Steffie practically lived here from sixth grade to ninth grade."

Kathleen knew all this. The girl was way too familiar with Carson's family and home, yet there had been nothing Kathleen could have said without coming across as a whiny witch, which she was when it came to Stephanie Marlow. So she kept quiet.

"Mom wasn't as involved in Dad's practice in those days," Carson continued. "She was around a lot more because I was younger and my sister was still at home. It's only since I've been in high school that she's kept full-time hours."

"And so Stephanie adopted your family?"

"You could say that. She followed me around like a puppy, but I didn't mind. I mean, she's always been beautiful. When Steffie was thirteen, the modeling industry noticed her. It was also the first time I saw her mother really take an interest in her. She took her to New York, got her signed with an agency, took her to photo shoots. Steffie did catalog work for a while and was always flying off on weekends and long holidays to Texas or California or New York. When they dressed her up, she looked twenty."

And hot, Kathleen thought. The girl was stunning. What guy wouldn't have fallen for her? She said, "Did she get treated like she was twenty?"

"In every way." He rotated his shoulder, massaged his forearms. "By the time she was fourteen, she was into tranquilizers and alcohol."

Kathleen's mouth dropped open. "What did her mother do?"

"She never noticed." He offered a sardonic laugh. "Steffie was good at hiding it, though, so *no one* noticed."

"Did you?"

"She told me. We, um, sometimes drank together."

He grew quiet and Kathleen realized that every muscle in her body had gone rigid with tension. His story had taken on a life and she saw it clearly in her head like a noir movie—two kids testing their boundaries. She wondered what else they might have experimented with while they were alone. "Not at your house?"

"Never. Only at hers. Because by then, Steffie's mother was no longer interested in her career and was globe-trotting for weeks at a time. Steffie told me that her mother figured she'd launched her into life, gotten her a start in a career where she could make great money, and therefore, her job was done."

"Sounds cold."

He shrugged. "She was treating Steffie like an adult, except that she wasn't." He blew out a heavy sigh. "Then one night, Steffie called me. She had OD'd. My folks were off at a medical conference and I was alone—my sister had already left the nest. I ran all the way to her house and found her semiconscious. She was pretty out of it, but she begged me not to call 911. She said she was sorry, that it was an accident." He stopped talking abruptly.

"And you didn't call," Kathleen said matter-of-factly.

"My parents were doctors. I knew what to do. I did it."

Kathleen closed her eyes. Her whole body trembled as she realized what a serious and dangerous thing he'd done. "What if she'd—"

"Well, she didn't. She was pretty sick, though. I stayed all night and most of the next day too, until she was really okay. I took her to my house because I was afraid to let her out of my sight, and we watched movies until Mom and Dad came home. We waved and told them we were just hanging out. Mom ordered pizza and life went on."

Kathleen thought about all he'd told her. "*Was* it an accident?"

He shrugged. "She said it was an accident, but

at the time, she was pretty unhappy. And by not reporting it, well, it meant she wouldn't have to see a psychiatrist like she would've if she'd been brought to the hospital. But she swore to me she'd never make a mistake like that again—mixing the pills and booze. And so far she hasn't."

And she's used it to bind you to her all this time, Kathleen thought, but she said, "What if she does?"

"I'll call 911, like I should have the first time. But the point I'm making is that I'd be a good EMT. I don't know how to make my dad understand that."

"Maybe all you can do is just keep talking to him about it."

"Well, we'd better come to an agreement soon. I've got to get my schedule changed before August."

"Would it be so terrible to take the prep courses? It would make you even more ready for community college."

He looked aghast. "And give up partying? Give up messing around with my girl?" The kidding tone she was so used to crept into his voice, and his gaze grew mischievous. He was once again the Carson she knew best.

"That girl would be me, wouldn't it?"

He grinned. "None other."

"I'll give you special permission to study harder and longer."

He propelled himself across the space

between their two beanbag chairs and fell on top of her. "Never!"

"You're squashing me." She twisted, but she was helplessly pinned beneath him.

"Should I call a paramedic?" He didn't wait for her answer; he crushed his mouth against hers. Instantly, Kathleen was lost in a haze of heat, with the throb of her own blood running hot and hungry in her veins.

"You were a fabulous clown and everybody loved you," Raina said, standing over Hunter, who sat in a chair in her room having his clown makeup removed.

"But was I sexy?"

"Amazingly sexy. To me." She slathered cold cream on his forehead.

"Was it my red nose or my big feet that turned you on the most?"

She laughed and wiped wadded tissue over the melting mess of whiteface. "How could I choose? You'll just have to wonder."

"I think I scared one little girl. She took one look at me and started crying."

"You weren't nearly as scary-looking then as you are now." She stepped aside, and he looked in the mirror and feigned passing out. "Come on. Sit up."

"If Stephen King saw me, he could write a book."

"Quiet." Raina worked until the wastebasket was filled with tissue and Hunter's face was red and shiny from being rubbed.

"Is there any skin left?" he asked. "How do you girls take this stuff off every day?"

"Regular makeup removal is a snap. This is heavy-duty greasepaint." She stepped back. "I think I've gotten it all. Go wash your face and let me inspect you again."

He stood, ducked into the adjoining bathroom and returned in minutes with the front of his hair damp and a towel hanging around his neck. "All clean," he said. "Do I get a kiss for bravery?"

She complied gladly. "You smell like a girl," she teased.

"And to think I was going to give you a present before that crack."

"A present! I want my present."

He went to a duffel bag he'd brought and extracted a handful of thin necklaces that when snapped were chemically activated and glowed in the dark. "Left over from my clown giveaways. All different colors."

"I'm touched," Raina teased. She took a few of the necklaces and looped them over a bedside lamp. "Now you can find me in the dark."

He grinned, came back to the bed and leaned over her. "I'd rather feel my way to you."

She slugged him playfully.

He made a face, flopped backward onto her

bed, propped himself up on his elbows and cocked his head. "How's it going with you and your mother these days?"

Her smile faded. Trust Hunter to bring up the one subject she didn't want to talk about. "We coexist."

"How long are you going to stay mad at her?"

"I've got a lot to be angry about. A baby she gave up for adoption was something worth knowing, don't you think?"

"Maybe." He pulled her down to lie next to him and rolled to one side so that he was looking down at her on the bed. "A lot of women give up babies and never tell the families they go on to raise. It's their right. If Emma had tracked down your mom asking to meet her biological family, it would have made sense to tell you, but Emma didn't. And if she didn't want to know and your mom didn't want to tell—"

"But we're sisters! I should know that I have a blood sister."

"Why?"

His question stopped her cold. "Because," she sputtered. "Just because." She turned her head. "There's the bone marrow thing," she said, looking back at him. "It probably saved her life because it came from a blood relative."

"A great gift you gave her. That's terrific. You should be proud and happy to have done it."

"So what's your point?"

"I just don't get why you're so mad at your mother. If *you* had been the one needing bone marrow and she refused to tell you about a sister, I could understand it. But you weren't. You discovered you had a sister, and you helped save her life, which pleased you. Why are you angry at Vicki?"

"She lied about our father too. She let me believe that he deserted us."

"He did."

Agitated, Raina sat up. "All my life, I've been 'I,' an only child. All your life, you've had Holly, a sibling. You're a 'we.' Now I'm a 'we' also. It takes getting used to. And my father never even had a chance to know about me. Mom never told him!"

Hunter looked thoughtful. "So deep down, you think if he'd known about you, he'd have stuck around. Is that right?"

Maybe that was what she had thought. She was amazed that Hunter had put a name to her anger so quickly.

"He was a burned-out druggie. What difference would having another child have made to him when he never accepted responsibility for the first one?"

"It might have," she snapped, hot tears stinging her eyes.

"Hey, hey . . . I don't want to make you cry." He took her in his arms and she stiffened. "I was just talking you through it."

She sniffed.

"Are you keeping in touch with Emma?"

"I—I'd like to. I'm not sure I know how. She's married and . . . and . . . we don't have much in common."

"You have your bone marrow."

"She's already thanked me for that. Truth is, I don't know how to be a sister."

He cuddled her. "You'll learn."

"I don't know when. We live five hundred miles apart. You grew up with Holly. You're a part of each other."

"Scary, isn't it?" he joked. He smoothed Raina's hair, cupped her chin and gazed deeply into her eyes. "It takes more than bloodlines to be related. It takes work and commitment."

"And my mother isn't interested in being related to Emma at all."

"But you are. And something will happen to bring the two of you closer together. I don't know what, but something will come along. Until it does, keep e-mailing her and phoning. She'll grow to love you like I do. Not as much," he added, kissing the tip of Raina's nose. "But trust me, she will love you for more than donating your bone marrow to her."

six

"This summer's going by way too fast," Holly told her friends. It was Saturday, and they were relaxing poolside in lounge chairs under big umbrellas at Raina's town house complex.

"Way too fast," Kathleen mumbled dreamily, half asleep.

"School starts in four weeks," Holly said.

Raina threw a towel at her. "Don't spoil the day. I'm not ready to go back." Truth be told, she wasn't ready for Hunter to leave. Their senior year would start the last week in August, but because he'd gotten a jump start on college last winter, he wouldn't head off to Indiana until after Labor Day. She was dreading it.

"Aren't you grouchy?" Holly said. "I'm looking forward to being a senior. Queen of the Hill. Top dog."

"I can't wait to graduate and go far, far away," Raina said.

"How far? I thought we were all going to try for the same college."

Kathleen raised her head. "University of South Florida for me. It's where Mom can afford to send me." The local university was on the north side of Tampa.

"I was hoping we'd all go to Florida or Florida State," Holly said, disappointed, for they had talked for years about attending the same college and being roommates. "They're both far enough away that my parents won't be looking over my shoulder every minute."

Kathleen shrugged. "I have to live at home. Dorm living costs too much." She didn't add that she also felt an obligation to stay nearby for her mother's sake. A recent flare-up of Mary Ellen's multiple sclerosis had laid her low, and despite her support system, Mary Ellen had needed Kathleen more than ever. Her form of MS—relapsing-remitting—was like that; it came and went, but the relapses could be incapacitating. Kathleen said, "The bright side is that Carson plans to go to college around here too." She didn't mention the community college, which was still being discussed by his parents.

"And I'm looking at colleges closer to Hunter," Raina said.

"Since when? What about the plans *we* made?" Holly was surprised, then irritated.

"Plans change."

"When were the two of you going to say something to me? This just stinks!"

Raina and Kathleen exchanged glances. Raina said, "Holly, it's not a conspiracy against you. It's just the way things are working out."

"Money's a real issue for me," Kathleen said.

"No," Holly said coolly. "You both have boyfriends and they're dictating your plans."

No one spoke.

"I'm right, aren't I?" By now Holly was worked up and getting angrier by the moment.

"It's a combination of things," Kathleen said. "Yes, Carson will stay in Tampa. But the money—"

"Spare me." Holly turned to Raina. "And you?"

"All I've ever wanted is Hunter," Raina said quietly. "You've always known that."

Holly felt something inside her explode. "And how about the God stuff? What are you doing about that, Raina? How will you fit into his life if he becomes a pastor? Do you think he wants to drag along an atheist for the rest of his life?" Holly saw that her words were hitting Raina like rocks, but she didn't care. She was usually the one in the middle, smoothing over Raina's ruffled feathers or shoring up Kathleen's sagging ego, and now they were both heading off in different directions without giving her feelings a single thought.

Kathleen attempted to defuse Holly. "Look, it's not the end of the world. You're smart, Holly.

Your grades are in the stratosphere, and you placed in the top five in our school on the ACT last year. You'll be accepted to any college you choose. Pick one. Go for the gold."

"I want to be with my friends," Holly said through gritted teeth. "What's crystal clear is that my best friends don't want to be with me."

"That's not true. We have our whole senior year together. And the rest of the summer too. We're all Pink Angels—"

Holly stood up. "Don't throw me crumbs. I'm out of here." She grabbed her towel and stalked toward the gate.

Kathleen jumped up. "Don't leave."

Holly unlatched the gate without a backward glance.

"I brought you. Don't you want a ride home?"

"I'll call my mommy like a good little girl!" Holly shouted over her shoulder. "She'll be thrilled that I need her."

She slammed out of the gate and Kathleen turned to Raina, who still hadn't recovered from Holly's verbal assault. Kathleen dropped onto the chair beside Raina. "She . . . she didn't mean all the things she said. She was just upset. She'll get over it."

"She was right, though." Raina's voice sounded thick. "What's Hunter going to do with a girl like me?"

"He's going to love you, as he has for years."

"We're miles apart on a few big issues. They're like a mountain between us. He needs someone who's more like him, who can see the world through his eyes."

"He needs *you*," Kathleen said emphatically.

"You're kind to say so, but I'll just drag him down."

Kathleen stopped offering protests.

Raina picked up her towel. "Let's go back to my room. We'll make some popcorn—" Her voice cracked and Kathleen's heart went out to her. Raina steadied herself. "Do you think Holly will stay angry at us?"

"No way," Kathleen said as they walked. "It's not in her nature."

Kathleen was wrong. Holly stewed in her anger for the rest of the week, going so far as to ask her mother to drive her to and from the hospital so that she wouldn't have to ride with Raina and Kathleen.

"Did you all have a falling-out?" her mother asked.

"Can't I have some privacy on this?"

"I'm not prying. I'm just asking if it's something you'd like to talk about."

"No, Mother, I don't want to talk about it."

Evelyn didn't ask again, but she did allow Holly to drive herself to the hospital two days the following week when she didn't need the car. For that Holly was grateful, because her anger had morphed into deep hurt over Raina and Kathleen's betrayal. She went online and searched for colleges for herself. She didn't need her friends. It was time for the Three Musketeers to go their separate ways.

Holly didn't even cave when Kathleen called and asked if they could go shopping together for school clothes. "I've saved enough to buy some things, and you have a fashion eye and I don't," Kathleen said enticingly.

"Sorry, I'm busy," Holly told her.

"We could go another day."

"Maybe Raina will go with you."

"Holly . . . ," Kathleen chided.

"Got to run," Holly said, and hung up. Then she cried. Only her pride was standing in the way of her being with her friends—*former* friends, she told herself. Yet she couldn't seem to get over the hurt.

"You going to stay mad at them forever?" Hunter asked one evening, standing in the doorway of her room.

"Maybe," Holly answered, knowing he was asking because Raina had urged him to.

"Not very mature."

She stuck out her tongue at him. "They hurt my feelings and I can do whatever I want. Go away."

He did.

Two weeks before school started, she received an e-mail from Shy Boy.

SHY BOY: Are you still speaking to me?
HOLLY: Yes, but I'm pretty sick and tired of you toying with me. Either we meet or you stop contacting me altogether. It's been six months already!

She knew she was taking a chance, but at the moment that she hit the Send button, she didn't care. She was through being so nice to everybody. All that her niceness got her was everybody walking all over her, or taking her for granted.

The next day, Shy Boy responded:

You're right. We need to meet. When and where?

* * *

"I wish I could tuck myself into your suitcase and go with you," Raina told Hunter with a sigh.

They were alone down by the pool in her complex late one night. The moon scattered fractured light that looked like pale jewels across the surface of the water. They had been swimming, but were now sitting side by side on towels spread on the concrete. The warmth of the day's sun, long gone, seeped through the terry cloth.

"We'd never get away with it. At my college, coeds are strictly segregated in the dorms." He said it lightly, but she knew he was telling her the hard truth. He was leaving. She was staying. He put his mouth on her shoulder and sucked the moisture left on her skin by their swim.

Shivers shot up her back. "I'd be quiet as a mouse. No one would know."

"I'd know."

Her heart was heavy. School started for her in a week. One week later was when he'd leave. "I don't know what I'll do."

"Enjoy your senior year. You're doing that Pink Angels credit thing again, aren't you?"

"Yes. So is Kathleen. I don't know about Holly." She sighed. "I don't know much about your sister these days. She's still in a snit."

"It won't last forever."

"It's been almost three weeks already. Kathleen couldn't even lure her into the mall."

He pulled Raina into his lap, cradling her in his arms. "She'll get over it," he said. "But I'm not getting over wanting to kiss you."

She smiled up at him. "Don't let me stand in your way."

He kissed her cheeks, her forehead, her chin, tangled her hair in his big hands and finally, when every pore on her skin felt on fire, he kissed her long and deep on her mouth, sending fiery darts into her heart. Into her mind. Into her very soul.

* * *

Holly discovered that the biggest problem with being mad at her friends was having no one to talk to when something wonderful happened. Shy Boy had agreed to meet her before the Pink Angels awards ceremony that Thursday night. She was proud of herself for thinking of it. The hospital was a very public place, and meeting right before the ceremony meant that she really did have an excuse to duck away if they didn't mesh, up close and personal. Plus no one would be the wiser, meaning her parents, if they saw her talking to some boy in the lobby before the event.

With only days left before the ceremony, she could hardly wait. Shy Boy—she still didn't know his name—had sent her e-mails on and off for months, and now she was finally going to meet him. *He'd better be worth the wait,* she told herself as she drove home from the hospital on Tuesday. She itched to pick up her cell phone and call Kathleen and Raina. She quelled the urge. If the meeting went well, she'd forgive them and tell them everything. If it didn't go well, she'd never tell them. Why humiliate herself?

Holly pulled into the garage, hopped out of the car and bounded into the house. "Mom, I'm home."

"Up here," Evelyn called. "I'm in your room."

Holly rolled her eyes. *Now what?* Were there dust bunnies under her bed? Had she forgotten to do something her mother had asked before she'd gone off that morning? She took the stairs two at a time and skidded to a halt in her doorway, where her mother was standing stone-faced, holding a small three-ring binder—the binder where Holly had stashed six months' worth of printed-out e-mails from Shy Boy.

seven

"NEVER LEAVE THE cash register unattended."
Kathleen was talking to Bree Sinclair, the girl
who would take her place part-time in the gift
shop once she returned to school.

"I'd never do that," Bree said, her big blue
eyes looking serious.

She was younger than Kathleen, a sopho-
more in a high school in an older part of the city,
and had been with the Pink Angels program all
summer. Now that school was starting, the gift
shop would need more hands. Bree had an out-
going, perky personality that reminded Kathleen
of Holly in many ways—when Holly was speaking to her.

"This is an inventory sheet, and Mrs. Nesbaum expects us to do an in-depth product count
once a month. It's a pain, but it's necessary." The
older woman loved Kathleen and often left her
in charge of the shop. Kathleen was going to miss
the job, and the money it brought her too. Once
school resumed, she'd be assigned elsewhere for

her credit work. She would keep the gift shop job two Saturdays a month, however.

"This is the refrigerated unit, where we hold the floral bouquets until someone comes to deliver them." The tall unit was at the back of the shop and contained the morning's delivery of live arrangements from local florists.

"I've done that before," Bree said. "The floral cart has a bad wheel, so it's like wrestling with an alligator to make it go the way you want."

The girl even sounded like Holly.

"Can I have some help here?"

Kathleen spun at the sound of the irritated voice and saw Stephanie Marlow standing at the glass-topped counter, a package of candy in her hand. Kathleen's heart thudded and her stomach twisted into a knot. She forced a smile. "You're home. Carson said you were away."

"And he told me you were working here when I saw him last night."

The information was given to unnerve Kathleen, and it had the desired effect. "Yes, I'm in charge of the shop."

"How charming. Did you miss me all summer?"

Not at all. "We managed."

Stephanie dropped coins into Kathleen's hand, careful not to touch her. "I was in Paris, New York, Hawaii and Brazil. My mother's family lives in Brazil, you know."

"So Carson's said."

"But I'm home now. Ready for my last year at Bryce. With Carson."

Kathleen put the candy into a bag and handed it over.

"And I'll be looking forward to the first party of the year. Someone always throws one, you know."

Kathleen felt her blood boil at Stephanie's veiled reference to the Christmas party where she'd seen Stephanie and Carson kissing—a kiss he swore she had initiated. Kathleen concentrated on what Carson had shared about a fourteen-year-old Stephanie mixing pills and booze, in an attempt to conjure up sympathy for the girl. But one look at Stephanie's contemptuous expression and her attempt failed.

"Don't work too hard." Stephanie sashayed out of the shop.

"Yikes! Who was that?"

Startled, Kathleen remembered that Bree was standing right behind her. "Just a girl I know."

"She's beautiful."

"She may be pretty, but she acts like a b—" Kathleen stopped short.

Bree giggled. "I know the type. Why doesn't she like you?"

"A guy." Kathleen was becoming flustered. Why did she allow Stephanie to rattle her so?

"Let me guess. He likes you better than her. Am I right?"

"So he tells me. I've wondered *why* often enough, but I think it's true."

Bree laughed. "Well, that's no mystery. You're nice and she isn't. Girls that pretty think they can get anything they want just because of their looks."

"You've figured that out already?"

"My father's a psychiatrist. I know a lot of that stuff."

"Is that why you're a Pink Angel?" Kathleen recalled that that was why Carson had been in the program when they'd first met—because his parents had their practice at this hospital.

"Partly. I needed to get out of the house too. My grandmother is living with us now, and she's slipping into Alzheimer's—where no one can visit." Bree's sunny expression turned cloudy.

"I—I'm really sorry."

Bree shrugged. "Mom's trying to take care of her at home." She shook her head. "It's a mess." She brightened. "Forget I said anything. Show me the rest of what I'm going to be doing in this job."

Kathleen returned to explaining her duties, but her brain wouldn't let go of what Bree had told her. Bree's life was difficult too, and not even having a doctor in her family could save her grandmother from the dark places she was entering. No more than Kathleen could reverse her mother's journey into advancing MS.

* * *

"What did you think they were going to do, sis? Let it slide? You had an e-mail correspondence going with a complete stranger. The guy could be a serial killer, for all you know." Hunter was standing over Holly in her room.

She sat cross-legged on her bed, a pile of tissues beside her. "Th-they didn't have to be so mean about it."

"*Mean?* How do you figure that? You were stuffing the e-mails between your mattress and box spring! You knew what you were doing was wrong. Admit it."

"I just sat through an hour-long lecture from Mom and Dad," Holly wailed. "I don't need another one from you!"

Hunter raked a hand through his hair and sat beside her.

Holly blew her nose, added the tissue to the heap and grabbed another one. "And he's not a serial killer either."

"How do you know that? You don't even know his name!"

"He had his reasons," Holly insisted.

"Name them."

She threw herself to one side and cried harder. Of course she couldn't think of any at the moment. "H-he was clever and smart and we talked about everything! I *like* him, Hunter."

Hunter sighed deeply and put his hand on

her arm sympathetically. "Listen, little sister, you're too trusting. Any guy who hides his identity for six months from a girl he says he likes is up to no good." Hunter's tone was serious enough to make Holly look up. "The world's full of evil, Holly. Don't think that just because you believe in God and go to church every Sunday, evil can't touch you. It can."

She righted herself. "Is that what you've learned in that Christian college? Evil walks among us? All you have to do is turn on the news to know that. Shy Boy isn't evil! He's just . . . well . . . *shy*, that's all."

"Sheez . . . talking to you is like talking to a wall."

He started to stand, but she grabbed his arm. She didn't want to be alone just then, and Hunter's company beat her parents coming in to give her another blast. "Isn't God supposed to protect us?"

"Why should he when we do something stupid?"

She grimaced. "You already sound like a preacher."

He hauled her to her feet and put his arms around her. "Here's a hug. You need one."

She buried her face in the front of his shirt, pulling back when a new wave of tears threatened. "Thank you for the hug."

"So what's your punishment?"

"Grounded until further notice. I can't leave

the house except to go to school when it starts. No car privileges. No TV for a week. No computer activity, especially e-mail or Net surfing." Her eyes widened. "You've got to do me a favor!"

Hunter eyed her skeptically. "Like what?"

"Dad nixed the Pink Angels awards event Thursday night too. I—I told Shy Boy that I'd meet him in the hospital lobby before it started. Please e-mail him for me and tell him I can't make it."

Hunter threw up his hands and backed away. "Oh no. I'm not telling this guy anything."

"But I can't go." Fresh tears brimmed and spilled over. "I begged Dad, but he wouldn't budge. I'm getting an award and I can't even go pick it up."

"I'll get the award for you, but I won't do the other."

She threw herself at him. "Oh, please, Hunter! Just on the outside chance that I'm right about this guy and everyone else isn't."

"Can't you ask Raina? Or Kathleen?"

"You know we're not speaking."

"And whose fault is that?"

She shook her finger at him. "Don't start. I was wrong to shut out my friends, but I did and now I can't just ask for a favor because I need them. How lame is that?"

"You can call—"

"Did I mention that I've lost phone privileges too? I really need you to do this for me. Please."

Hunter gave a disgusted growl. "If I do it, I'm

going to tell him exactly what I think of him for leading my sister on."

She started to protest, but one look at Hunter's face changed her mind. Subdued, she said, "Thank you."

He left her room and she threw herself across her bed and cried some more.

Holly was moping around her room on Saturday when someone knocked. "Friend or foe?" she asked.

"Friends," Raina and Kathleen said in unison.

Holly grabbed the doorknob and jerked open the door. She threw herself into their arms. "Oh my gosh! I'm so happy to see you two!"

The girls staggered back. "Don't squeeze us to death!" Raina said.

Holly backed off, glanced down the hall. "How did you get past Cerberus?"

They gave Holly a blank look until Kathleen finally grinned and said, "You mean the three-headed dog that guards the entrance into Hades in Greek mythology?"

"That's the one."

"Don't be so dramatic, girlfriend," Raina said. "Your mother was quite nice. Although she did set the kitchen timer."

"Come in," Holly said. "Excuse the mess, but I've been a prisoner in here for days." She scraped a pile of books, CDs and clothes off her bed and motioned for them to sit.

Kathleen held up a brown paper sack. "We brought snacks and your award from the Pink Angels program. Everybody missed you."

"What did you tell Sierra?"

Raina said, "That you'd had a run-in with the law, and the law won."

"Don't joke."

"Unavoidable circumstances," Kathleen said. "She was sorry." She handed Holly the bag. "Comfort food."

Holly rummaged inside and found two jars of ice cream toppings, a bag of candy, a box of crackers and two boxes of cookies. At the bottom she saw her award, and lifted it out. The plaque read BEST TEAM SPIRIT, JUNIOR VOLUNTEER OF THE YEAR. She'd been awarded top honors. "And I missed the whole thing! That just stinks!"

"I grabbed it out of Hunter's hands and told him we wanted to bring it, and that he wasn't to say a word about it to you," Kathleen said.

"He didn't." A lump clogged Holly's throat. "I—I'm sorry for the way I've been acting the past couple of weeks. Forgive me?"

"All forgotten," Raina said, and Kathleen nodded enthusiastically. "I've asked your mother if I can pick you up on the first day of school, and she said okay."

"Really?" Holly brightened.

Mercifully, neither of her friends asked about Shy Boy, which relieved Holly because she couldn't talk about it yet. She ripped open a cookie box. "Help yourselves and tell me everything that's happened since the hostile takeover of my brain by my pride, making me forget just what fabulous friends I have."

After they left, Holly ventured downstairs, sulking past her parents in the living room, where her father sat at his desk paying bills and her mother worked on the sofa doing needlepoint. The doorbell rang. "I'll get it," Holly said.

Without comment, her father followed behind her, which made her furious. Did he think she'd bolt down the street once the front door was unlatched?

She opened the door and faced a teen boy with sharp features. He was tall and impossibly skinny, with a full head of wild, curly black hair that hung in shaggy ringlets above bright green eyes.

"Can I help you?" Mike asked from behind Holly.

The boy's gaze, locked on Holly, shifted up to her father. "Hello, sir. My name is Chad Kyriakidis. I think you know me by my e-mail name, Shy Boy."

eight

HOLLY FROZE. *This was Shy Boy?* He wasn't at all what she'd expected.

"Hello, Chad," Mike Harrison said. "Is there something I can do for you?"

Holly was speechless and also embarrassed. This wasn't at all how she'd envisioned—a hundred times over—meeting him.

"I—um—I would like to talk to you, sir. I'd like to apologize for getting Holly in trouble. I'd like to explain myself."

Holly could feel her father's displeasure but was heartened when he said, "Yes. Holly's mother and I would like to hear what's been going on."

For the first time, Holly realized that they had not trusted her explanation of an innocent e-mail flirtation. Her face felt hot with color. She stepped aside, and Chad followed her and her father into the living room, where Chad was introduced to her mother. Evelyn nodded politely, but Holly could see by her parents' expressions that Chad had a whole lot of persuading to do if he was ever going to win over the Doubtful Duo.

Chad sat on the edge of an overstuffed chair across from the sofa where her parents settled. She felt like excess baggage but eventually took the chair at her father's desk. Chad licked his lips, stared down at his hands clasped on his knees. He looked up. "I'm really sorry about making trouble for Holly. I never meant to do that."

No one said anything.

Chad continued. "I had no idea of the trouble she was in until Hunter e-mailed me. He told me he was her brother before he lit into me."

Her parents looked over at Holly. "I asked him to," Holly said boldly. "So don't get mad at him."

"I know the way I've handled our friendship is crazy," Chad said, turning attention back on himself. "But even though we've only ever e-mailed each other, I've really grown to like her. A lot."

Holly felt her cheeks grow warm again.

"Why did you pick Holly?" Mike asked. "Do you go to the same high school?"

"No. I—um—I'm homeschooled. I live over in Tarpon Springs." That was a beautiful Greek fishing village about forty miles from Tampa, on the Gulf of Mexico. Holly had been there years before, visiting with her family. She remembered watching from a glass-bottom boat as divers harvested sponges. "I have seen her around the hospital when she helps on the kid floors."

Now Holly was baffled. She had never seen Chad.

"Are you a volunteer at the hospital too?" Evelyn asked.

"Not exactly." Chad shook his mane of curly hair, as if clearing his head. "Let me back up. I got hold of her e-mail address at the hospital. It was an accident; no one gave it to me. Someone named Kathleen e-mailed Holly some stuff from the medical library last year, and I just happened to see the address when I was doing some research at the same terminal."

"I did a report for biology, and Kathleen e-mailed me some articles," Holly explained. "She was assigned to the medical library then."

"I already wanted to know her better but didn't know how to approach her, so I just started e-mailing."

"Seems devious," Mike said.

"There were large time gaps between your e-mails," Evelyn said. "Why was that?"

Holly squirmed because now he knew that her parents had read *every* word of their exchanges, yet she was glad her mother had asked the question. Holly burned to know the answer. This whole scene could have been avoided if he'd only met with her ages ago.

"Everybody uses the computer at my house. No privacy."

"Why was privacy necessary?"

Chad looked miserable. "I didn't want her to know everything there is to know about me."

That's honest, Holly thought. *But scary.*

"Sounds strange," Mike said. "What are you hiding?"

Chad took a deep breath. "I—um—I have CF, cystic fibrosis. That's why I go to the hospital so much. It's a lousy disease. All my life, I've wanted to be normal. I've wanted a normal girl to *like* me. A pretty girl." He cut his eyes to Holly. "Pretty like Holly. Someone who won't be turned off or freaked out by coughing and respiratory therapy and all the medical stuff that goes along with CF. I had hoped that Holly would like me through my e-mails enough to not be grossed out when she met the real me.

"Instead I got her into a ton of trouble, and so I've probably made her hate me instead. I'm sorry, Holly. Very, very sorry."

"The summer has passed so quickly," Carson's mother, Teresa, told Kathleen in her lilting Spanish accent. They were standing in the magnificent kitchen washing vegetables for the cookout that Dr. Kiefer was setting up on the back patio. Carson was outside with his father.

"I guess this is the last picnic of the summer,"

Kathleen said. It was the Saturday before Labor Day, and the Kiefers were having a few couples over for dinner. Carson had asked Kathleen to come so he wouldn't be stuck in a crowd of boring adults. He'd said, "We'll watch some movies, maybe get in some lip-lock time." Of course she'd agreed.

"Yes, Christopher and I are on call on Monday, so we had to move our party up. We're very glad you could come."

"Me too." Kathleen thought back to the previous Labor Day, when Stephanie had shown up uninvited, and she hoped there wouldn't be a repeat appearance.

"So you've been in school a week. How is it going?"

"There's a ton of freshmen and everybody looks lost. Cummings is huge. Carson says Bryce Academy is a whole lot smaller. The difference between public and private, I guess."

"That and a wheelbarrow full of money," Teresa said with a laugh. "I must tell you something."

Kathleen braced herself.

"You have been good for our son, Kathleen."

The compliment took Kathleen by surprise. "You think so?"

"Do not be modest. It is true. Carson has always been, how shall I say? Not totally manageable. Since the two of you have been dating, he is less wild. More centered. I give you credit for that."

The flattery made Kathleen blush deeply. "H-he's kind to me."

"Ah, this is good to know. Kindness is a good trait. I would not put up with anyone who was not kind to me." Teresa glanced out the window, let her gaze rest on her husband and smiled. "Like father, like son." She turned back to Kathleen. "What do you think of Carson's idea to become an EMT?"

Kathleen's stomach tightened. She wasn't prepared for this conversation. Choosing her answer carefully, she said, "I think he'd be very good at it. He's good with people. He likes the excitement it would bring. And the variety. He's dedicated too. Plus I think he likes medicine more than he lets on. Yes, he'd make a wonderful EMT."

Teresa tipped her head, studied Kathleen for a moment. "This is what I have told his father. A child should be encouraged to follow a dream. This is why I am a doctor, because it was something I had always wanted. My family let me believe I could do it, although we had little money to send a girl to university. Carson should be able to do as he wishes. He is young and he can experiment until he finds the right fit."

"He told me his dad backed off on forcing

him to take some of his college prep classes this year."

"Yes." Teresa's eyes twinkled. "I checked into what courses were absolutely necessary for him to graduate, enter community college and be acceptable for the EMT program. Then I suggested a senior year schedule to both Carson and Chris that was agreeable."

The confession proved to Kathleen what she'd already surmised—that Carson's easy charm had been given to him with his mother's DNA.

"Where's your brother?" Holly's father asked as he walked into the kitchen, adjusting his necktie.

Holly, sitting at the kitchen table, had her nose buried in the Sunday comics as she answered. "He got a call from his boss, who said the morning guy was sick and couldn't open the restaurant, and would Hunter please open and let the cooks in, and he'd take over as soon as he could."

"Hunter said Friday was his last day on the job." Mike sounded irritated. Attendance at Sunday morning's family breakfast before church was mandatory.

Evelyn placed a fresh stack of pancakes on her husband's plate. "Just eat, hon. Hunter will join us as soon as he can, I'm sure."

Hunter was leaving for college on Tuesday,

and no one was looking forward to his going. Mike was taking off from work to drive him to Indiana. Holly itched for the day when she would leave for college and personal freedom. She had to admit, though, that Shy Boy's visit and conversation with them had helped her situation a little. No one had spoken after he'd dropped the bombshell about his health. He'd spent days, even weeks at a time in the teen wing of Parker-Sloan, and she had never noticed him. She felt bad about it.

When Chad had left the house, he'd asked Holly's father for permission to call her and maybe e-mail her again too. Mike had said, "All right, but give it a couple of weeks."

This had shocked Holly, because she hadn't thought she'd have any privileges until Christmas. The downside for her was that she wasn't sure she wanted Chad to call or write her at all. He just wasn't what she'd hoped for all the months she'd been fantasizing about him. Just her luck—a guy finally liked her and he was sick with a terrible disease. She had read up on CF and knew it wasn't a pretty thing. CF patients had a malfunctioning pancreas that prevented food from being properly digested, and their lungs were clogged with thick secretions of mucus that had to be removed through special respiratory manipulations. *Ugh.* Chad had been correct—CF was a turnoff.

"Holly, you'd better get a move on. I don't want to be late for Sunday school."

Holly started. She'd been in deep concentration, and her father's words propelled her into motion. "On my way. Be right back."

She hustled upstairs, brushed her teeth, put on lipstick and ran to her room to find her Bible. She grabbed it and her purse, happened to look out the window and saw a police car turn into the driveway. *Now what?*

Her father beat her to the front door just as the doorbell rang. He opened the door and Holly saw three men on the porch—a uniformed cop and two men wearing suits. "Can I help you?" Mike asked.

"Mr. Harrison?" the man with wavy hair and brown eyes asked.

"Yes."

"I'm Detective Oscar Gosso, with the Tampa Police Department." He flashed a badge. "This is Sergeant Tim Carroll and Chaplain Jack Frederick."

Holly saw a small gold cross pinned to the chaplain's lapel.

"May we come in?" the detective asked.

Evelyn walked into the foyer from the kitchen drying her hands on a dish towel. "What's wrong?"

"These men want to talk to us."

Mike and Holly moved aside and the three

men stepped in, following her father into the living room. Holly's heart thudded. *Why had the police come?*

"Do you have a son, Hunter Harrison?" the detective asked.

Evelyn looked alarmed. Mike nodded. "Has something happened to Hunter? Was there an accident?"

Holly's heart hammered and she felt queasy.

"Actually, sir," the detective said, his eyes darkly serious, "there's been a shooting at the restaurant where he works. There's no easy way to tell you this. I'm sorry, but he's been killed."

nine

TIME STOOD STILL—absolutely, totally still—for Holly. The past and the future lay trapped between heartbeats, snared in a tangle of micro-moments. In one heartbeat, she had a brother. By the next, she had none. She struggled to stay static between the beats, because to move forward was unthinkable, to go backward impossible. She was aware that time had resumed its flow, and that her heart had jump-started itself, when she heard her mother screaming.

Somehow Holly found herself and her mother sitting on the sofa. Her mother was sobbing and the chaplain was offering her a glass of water. Mike Harrison was still standing, but he looked sickly pale. "Are you sure it's our son?"

"His empty wallet and photo ID were found on top of him."

"Who found him?"

"The police. Your son had the presence of mind to trip the silent alarm."

"How did it happen?" Mike's voice was a croaked whisper.

"We'll be going over the security tape downtown, but it looks as if your son—"

"Hunter," Evelyn interjected. "His name is Hunter." Her voice broke.

Detective Gosso nodded. He looked sad. "Hunter . . . yes. It looks as if he unlocked the door and some guy came out of nowhere and shoved his way inside. He had a gun."

"Why?" Evelyn sobbed. "Why would someone shoot Hunter?"

Holly felt numb now, as if she were hearing questions and answers through a thick fog.

"It looks like the motive was robbery."

"Hunter always said they took the money away every night at closing."

"Not on Saturday nights, evidently. There's an unopened safe in the back office."

"He wouldn't have known how to open the safe," Mike said. "No employee has the combination. Only the manager and owner."

"The owner's on his way downtown to talk to us."

"So you're saying he was killed in cold blood." Mike's voice fell to a whisper.

Holly cringed, felt sick to her stomach. Everything felt surreal, like a nightmare, so vivid that she could smell the odor of stale coffee and cold fries from the fast-food restaurant where

Hunter had died. But it wasn't a dream. She could wake up from a dream. She saw tears trickle down her father's cheeks and clapped her hand over her mouth, afraid that she might throw up.

The detective glanced at the others. "The crime scene crew is examining the scene right now. We'll know more when they tender their report."

"We want to see our son," Mike said, clearing his throat.

"The medical examiner has taken Hunter to the morgue for an autopsy," Gosso told him.

"You said he was shot. Why does he have to go . . . there?"

"It's routine. We still have to examine the body, retrieve the bullet. For evidence," Gosso clarified.

"When can we see him?" Evelyn's voice sounded raspy.

"If you'll call the ME's office and give the name of the funeral home where you want Hunter sent, the ME will send him there when he releases the body. The funeral home will call you."

Evelyn broke down.

"How long will that take?" Mike demanded, looking coiled and edgy.

"Just a few days," Gosso said soothingly. "I'll ask the ME to expedite the case. I'll also give you my phone numbers." He reached into the breast pocket of his coat and extracted a business card. "I'm giving you my cell number too." He quickly scribbled on the card. "Call me anytime. Day or night."

The case. The body. An autopsy. The phrases whirled around in Holly's brain like a bad melody with clashing notes that didn't harmonize with her well-ordered world. Boys like Hunter didn't get shot to death. Guys like Hunter, who'd never done anything bad to anyone, didn't get *murdered.* Just thinking the word made her queasy again.

Holly's mother let out a wrenching sob. "You'll catch him, won't you? Please tell me you'll catch the person who did this."

The detective's eyes grew hard. "We'll catch him, Mrs. Harrison. You have my word." His gaze held Evelyn's, and she looked visibly strengthened by his pledge.

Agitated, Mike asked, "What do we do now? How do you expect us to sit around waiting, doing nothing?"

"Stay home," Gosso said. "Take your phone off the hook."

Sergeant Carroll added, "News of the shooting went out on the police scanner. The press will be calling. You might want to be ready for that."

His words shocked and infuriated Holly.

What right did a bunch of reporters have to intrude on their family at a time like this?

"We won't talk to them," Mike thundered, echoing Holly's thoughts.

"Just be prepared for it to go on the six o'clock news," the sergeant said.

Holly blanched as the horror of it all sank in. In only a few hours, the whole city would know about their very private loss. Her tears dried as she visualized the press nosing around her house. *The six o'clock news.* She hated them already.

"I won't let them on my property," Mike insisted.

Holly didn't know how much longer the police and the chaplain stayed, but the second they were gone, she fell to her knees in front of her mother. "I—I have to borrow your car."

Evelyn's eyes, red and swollen, stared at her in disbelief. "You can't be serious."

"I have to, Mom. Please. I can't just let her hear about it on the news . . . you know that, don't you?"

Evelyn's nod was almost imperceptible.

"You can't leave the house." Mike sounded aghast at Holly's request.

Evelyn looked up at him, held his gaze. "She has to, Mike. Take my car, Holly. The keys are on the hook by the kitchen door."

"She's too upset to drive—" Mike started.

Holly stood. "I have to do this, Daddy. Please understand."

He studied her hard. Her heart thumped, but her hands were rock steady. He gave a curt nod and Holly ran from the living room.

Fortunately, traffic was light as she wove her way down side streets and through quiet neighborhoods. Inside the houses, people were unaware that there had been a shift in the universe and that nothing would ever be the same again for Holly and her family and friends.

She turned into the town house complex, made her way to the street where Raina lived. She slowed, her heart pounding. *Keep it together,* she told herself. *Just a little bit farther.* Holly parked, rested her forehead on the steering wheel and took in great gulps of air. She turned off the car's engine, got out and walked up to Raina's door, her knees rubbery, her heart thudding with dread. In a few minutes, the universe would collapse for Raina too. It wasn't fair. Holly would take away the sunshine, alter the course of her friend's life forever. She rang the bell.

Raina opened the door, saw Holly and smiled. "Hey there, girlfriend!"

Holly watched the smile fade and concern stamp itself on Raina's pretty face.

"What's wrong?" Raina looked alarmed.

Holly felt her face crumble inward. "Somebody shot Hunter, Raina. Someone killed my big brother."

Raina staggered backward, as if Holly had shoved her. "That's a lie. That can't be true." She sank to her knees in the foyer.

Holly crouched in front of her, let Raina search her face with stunned and disbelieving eyes. As the truth of Holly's words sank in, Raina gagged, almost retched, hugged herself tightly, rocked back and forth on her knees. She began to wail. Holly dissolved into sobs. She reached out and put her arms around her friend and they clung to each other, fighting to stay out of the abyss that threatened to swallow them whole.

Holly couldn't comfort Raina, and Raina couldn't comfort her. They needed Hunter. He would help them to be all right. But Hunter was no more. He had disappeared into the vortex of nonexistence, one beautiful, clear, summer Sunday morning, when the evil he had once warned Holly about had come calling.

ten

KATHLEEN COULDN'T STOP crying. The news about Hunter came from Raina's mother via a phone call. Mary Ellen was crying when she brought the news to Kathleen, who was preparing to go to Raina's for an afternoon at the pool. Kathleen called Carson, and when she couldn't hold herself together on the phone, he came to her house.

"This is unreal," Carson kept saying while Kathleen sobbed. "It can't be happening."

"But it *did* happen. How could someone *do* that? Just walk up and kill somebody who'd done nothing wrong?"

"If I ever meet the guy in a dark alley . . . ," Carson said.

"It wouldn't bring Hunter back."

With Mary Ellen, they watched the evening news, on which Hunter's death was the lead story. "Oh, that poor family," Mary Ellen said, crying openly. "What a terrible thing. Have you talked to Holly yet?"

Kathleen shook her head. "I've called her and Raina both, but their lines are always busy, so I'll bet they've unplugged them. Their cell phones go straight to voice mail, so I know they've got them turned off too. I don't blame them. How can they talk about it yet? It's too horrible."

The TV reporter said that police were going over a surveillance tape that soon would be released to the public, and that the restaurant was offering a large reward for the perpetrator's capture. "Maybe someone will recognize the scum," Carson said.

"This is just too sad." Mary Ellen, back in her wheelchair since her latest flare-up of MS, shook her head and left the room.

Kathleen watched her mother go. "I'm worried about Mom."

"Why?"

"Stress causes problems for her."

"No one can lead a stress-free life."

"But the less stress, the better." Kathleen sighed. "Don't you see? This is bringing up all her bad memories from her and Dad's car wreck. I can tell it's affecting her."

Carson slid his arms around Kathleen and kissed her temple. "I liked Hunter. And if there's anything you want me to do to help your mother, you or your friends, tell me."

"The next few weeks are going to be really

hard for all of us. Just be with me through all of it," she said.

"There's no place else I want to be."

Holly felt as if their house had been invaded.

Pastor Eckloes came Sunday afternoon and stayed for hours. The elders came on Monday, and then people from the congregation showed up with food. Not that she or her mother or dad ate much of anything. Food stuck in her throat and she could hardly swallow. No one knew how to comfort them. Many people wanted to pray with the family, except that Holly didn't feel like praying. She just wanted everyone to leave them alone.

She hid in her room whenever she could. But the loneliness got to her quickly and she usually ended up pacing the upstairs hallway, listening to the murmurs from the floor below until she wanted to scream, "Go away!"

Everything in the house whispered Hunter's name and magnified their loss. In the bathroom Holly shared with him, she put his toothbrush, hairbrush, aftershave and razors into plastic bags and stowed them under the sink, out of sight. It helped to not have to constantly see his belongings, reminding her that he wasn't coming home.

In his bedroom, most of his things were packed in boxes and stacked along one wall, ready for the trip to college that would never come. He had stripped his bulletin board above his desk and now only a few lone thumbtacks remained in the cork. His closets were mostly empty and his bed was neatly made. Holly touched his pillow, where his head had lain only the night before, and cried.

She slept fitfully and woke with a start late Monday night to the sounds of weeping. She followed the sounds and found her mother sitting in the middle of Hunter's bed, holding his pillow and sobbing into it. Holly eased wordlessly onto the bed.

"It still smells like him," Evelyn said.

Holly buried her face in the pillow, where Hunter's scent lingered. "Why is this happening?" she whispered. "Why Hunter? Why us?"

Her mother didn't speak for a long time. When she did, she said, "All I know, Holly, is that almost nineteen years ago, God gave me a baby boy. A son. And now he's taken him away. In the cruelest and most terrible of ways, he's taken him from me."

Hunter's nineteenth birthday was coming up on September 30. Holly cried harder. All she wanted was for the pain to go away. She wanted her mother to comfort her, but Evelyn did not. And inside the shell of Hunter's room, Holly feared that she *could* not. Her mother had entered a dark place. She wouldn't be coming out anytime soon.

* * *

On Tuesday, Holly turned on her cell phone and found her voice mailbox crammed with messages from Kathleen, Carson, friends from the hospital and friends from school. There were none from Raina. Holly called Kathleen.

"I'm so relieved to hear from you!" Kathleen cried at the sound of Holly's voice.

"I'm sorry I haven't called sooner."

"It's okay. Please don't even think about it. I—I just needed to hear your voice."

Emotion clogged Holly's throat.

Kathleen asked, "Have you talked to Raina?"

"Not since . . . Sunday."

"She's not taking any calls. Carson and I went to her house on Monday, but her mother said she's in bad shape and her doctor was giving her sleeping meds and a few tranquilizers to help her through these next few days. Her mother is taking personal days off from work to take care of her."

"She was awfully upset," Holly said, alarmed by the information. At least Holly had her parents to go through the horror with her. Raina was alone. Of course Vicki was around, but they had been at odds for months.

"The TV stations are showing the surveillance tape. Have you seen it?"

"We're keeping the TV off, but I'll tell my folks." Holly's stomach heaved as she thought about actually seeing the person who'd done so much damage to their lives.

"Do you think you'll come back to school anytime soon?"

Holly hadn't thought once about school in days. "I don't know."

"Mom let me stay home again today, but I'll have to go tomorrow. I'm not looking forward to it."

"I—I have to go now."

"Sure," Kathleen said. "Call me again soon?"

"I will."

Holly hung up, rested her forehead in her hands and was startled when her cell chirped. She didn't recognize the number, but answered it anyway. If some reporter had gotten hold of her number, she was prepared to blast him or her.

"Hi. I—I wasn't sure you'd talk to me. I've called a couple of times, but didn't leave messages." The caller was Chad.

The memory of his face, his dark eyes and his unruly curly hair flashed. There might have been a time when she'd have been ecstatic to have a boy call her. Now it was inconsequential. "I've had my phone off for days."

"Holly . . . I'm really sorry. I don't know what to say."

"You aren't alone. Nobody knows what to say."

"If you ever want to talk . . . you know . . . just talk . . ."

She let the silence lengthen. "That's nice of you," she said finally. "I don't know what I want right now."

"Can I call you again? E-mail you?"

"I guess." She regretted not being nicer to him and added, "Thank you for calling. I—I know I have to start talking to people again. This was good practice."

"Anytime. My number's in your cell phone's memory now."

For reasons she couldn't explain, Holly did feel better after talking to Chad and Kathleen. She remembered what Kathleen had said about the videotape being shown on the news and went downstairs. The noon news was about to air. She turned on the TV, turned the volume down low and waited. Within the first few minutes of the broadcast, the tape ran. Her heart hammered as she watched the grainy footage, shown once in real time, then again in slow motion.

The image of a male wearing a torn T-shirt and jeans, with a baseball cap pulled low over his face, filled the television screen. The camera zoomed in on him, freeze-framing his head. Holly couldn't make out any of his features. How could anyone ever identify him? How could the cops ever find him if they had no better pictures than that?

"Turn it off."

Holly whirled and saw her mother standing in the doorway, her face an ashen, stony mask. Holly scrambled to turn off the set. "I—I . . ."

Her mother said nothing more, just turned on her heel and left the room.

Holly's face burned with shame, as if she'd been caught doing something awful. Tears threatened. She hadn't meant to hurt her mother. She'd only wanted to look at the force of evil that had destroyed her brother and devastated her family. She sank onto the sofa, buried her face in her hands and cried silently.

On Thursday, the coroner's office called to say that Hunter's body had been released to the funeral home for burial.

eleven

For Raina, all light had gone out of the world. Everything that had once been familiar and friendly loomed like treacherous icebergs, pulling her deep into waters that were icy cold and dark. She felt great gratitude toward the pills she was taking. They kept her brain foggy, her body languid and relaxed, just hovering on the verge of consciousness. If one dose began to wear off before it was time for another, she wept.

"These are just temporary," Vicki warned her as she gave Raina another dose. "Tomorrow you will taper off. One every eight hours. After that, one sleeping pill only at night. Then none."

Raina was too fractured to plead, but she was certain that she couldn't keep it together without the lovely little pills. By Friday morning, the prescription was finished and her retreat from reality was over. She was left to face her life without Hunter. Forever.

Vicki made her come down to breakfast,

which she couldn't eat. Vicki spread honey on a sliver of toast and handed it to Raina. "Eat it."

"I can't."

"You must. You'll need strength. Hunter's funeral is this afternoon. I assume you'll want to go. Naturally I'll go with you."

"Today?" Raina felt dismayed. She wasn't ready. She'd never be ready.

"Mike Harrison called last night to tell me. Only family and close friends are being invited to the graveside service. There will be a memorial service at the Harrisons' church afterward, and the whole community is expected to show up. Reporters will be there, I'm sure. If anyone shoves a mike in your face, kick them where it will hurt the most."

Raina nodded. She forced down the toast, went upstairs, took a long, hot shower, washed her hair and put on light makeup. She dressed in a soft floral-print dress that Hunter had loved. She brushed her hair until it shone like spun gold. She put on sunglasses. She did it all for Hunter . . . because it would be the last thing she could ever do for him.

Holly was seated with her parents at the burial site, under a canopy, when the invited guests began to arrive. The mahogany casket that held her brother sat on a raised platform, draped with a mantle of spring flowers. Holly clutched a box of tissue, watching Raina and her mother walk from their car. Behind them came Kathleen and Carson, pushing Mary Ellen's wheelchair over the bumpy ground. Three of Hunter's best friends from high school and three buddies from their church youth group were acting as pallbearers.

The cemetery looked beautiful, clipped and trimmed and bathed in sunlight. Bright splashes of flowers dotted the landscape, tributes to all who'd come before her brother. In the distance, she saw a small lake edged with tall rushes and grasses, a fountain in its center. The water sprayed upward to some mysterious rhythm; the droplets caught sunbeams and then splattered onto the surface, where they disappeared into the deep only to rise and shower again.

Holly was glad that her parents had opted for the small private burial. She was dreading the memorial service yet to come. How much more grief could she and her parents bear?

When everyone was gathered, Pastor Eckloes stepped forward and read Bible passages about life and death, hope and heaven. Holly's thoughts wandered. She'd attended church all her life, believed in what she'd been taught, never questioned it. Until now. Yes, the promise of heaven seemed glorious, but she could not understand why God had taken Hunter away from them.

She had overheard her mother challenging the pastor one afternoon at their house. "I thought God sends angels to protect his own. Where were Hunter's angels the day he was shot?"

"Hunter's angels had a different job that day—to carry him up to heaven," the pastor had answered.

Holly thought the image of winged angels bearing Hunter off a pretty one, but it brought her no understanding, no peace. Her brother had not deserved to die. God could have prevented it. He hadn't. It made no sense to her.

When the brief graveside service was over, Holly went to Raina and Kathleen. They hugged one another. Kathleen said, "This is so hard. So horrible."

"I'm just pretending he's away at college, like he planned," Holly said. "It's easier to lie to myself than to say he's never coming home again."

Raina said, "This is the worst day of my life."

Carson came up, put his arms around Kathleen and Holly. "Do the cops have any news?"

"Not that we've heard."

"They'll get the sorry scumbag."

"You sound like the detective who's in charge of the case," Holly said. "But why is it taking so long?"

Holly's father called her. "I really wish we

could go home. I don't want to go through another service," she told her friends.

"None of us do," Raina said. "It's just more of
the same nightmare."

"I'll call you both later," Holly said, and she
hurried off to ride to the huge brick church for a
second service, which would commemorate
Hunter's brief life.

"There certainly was a crowd," Mike said that
evening.

"Even people who hardly knew him or us,"
Holly said, feeling resentful about reporters she
thought had no business coming.

She sat with her parents at the kitchen table.
A few dishes of the many brought by friends and
neighbors had been heated, but no one had an
appetite. Evelyn picked at a salad and Holly
toyed with a bowl of soup.

"But a lot who did," Mike said. "A lot of people loved our boy."

Holly had looked over the crowd briefly, rec-
ognizing teachers and kids from school, and
many from the hospital—Sierra; Susan from the
pediatric cancer wing; Mrs. Graham; Carson's
parents; Betsy, the newborns' nurse Raina had
liked so much; even Mark Powell, the director of
volunteer services, including the Pink Angels
program. Seeing them jolted her back to a life

she'd almost forgotten. She'd been so swallowed up by what had happened that she hadn't thought about a world she'd soon have to rejoin.

"Mike, why did God take our son away from us?"

The look of sadness on her mother's face made Holly feel sick.

"Who can know the mind of God? His ways are beyond us."

"I don't want religious platitudes. I want to know why a boy who only wanted to serve God wasn't allowed to live. Why did God do that? God was supposed to take care of Hunter. He was supposed to keep him safe." Tears swam in Evelyn's eyes.

Holly's father looked weary, smaller somehow, as if he'd shrunk over the past days. "I don't know why. I just know that we still need God to get us through this. What do you want to do? Curse God and die? How would that honor Hunter? How would that help you?"

Evelyn locked gazes with him. Holly held her breath. Her mother's comments were valid. *Someone* owed them an explanation, a reason.

"In other words, God calls all the shots and we have no one to appeal his decisions to." Evelyn carefully folded her napkin, placed it on the table, pushed her chair backward. She stood and, without another word, left the room.

* * *

In her dream, Raina was floating in the pool at night. Stars glittered overhead and a soft tropical breeze rippled the water's surface. She felt warm, as liquid as the water itself.

"Hello, Raina."

The voice startled her. She righted herself. "Who's there?"

Hunter stepped from out of the darkness. Her heart leaped. "Hunter! You're all right!"

He crouched by the edge, laughing. "Of course I'm all right."

"You are! Oh, Hunter, I'm so happy to see you."

"Then why don't you swim over here and show me?"

She began to swim and swim and swim. The side of the pool never got closer. Soon she was gasping for air. "I—I don't know what's wrong." She looked up and saw that Hunter was standing.

"I've got to go, babe."

"But you can't! Don't leave me."

He stepped away, the smile still on his face. "I have to go."

"No! Don't go!" Raina thrashed in the water and it clung to her arms and legs like quicksand. "Hunter!"

Light streamed across Raina's face and she woke with a gasp and sat straight up. Her mother was opening the blinds on the window over Raina's bed.

"Honey, what's wrong?"

"I—I was having a dream. About Hunter. He was alive and . . . and . . ." Raina started to cry, covering her face.

Vicki sat on the bed, took Raina's wrists and pulled her hands away gently. "Listen to me. It was just a dream. You're going to have them from time to time."

"It was just so real." Raina noticed that her mother was dressed and beautifully groomed. "You're going to work?"

"I have to. And you have to go back to school. It's been ten days, Raina. Even Holly's gone back. Her mother told me this morning that she started back yesterday."

"I don't want to go."

"I know, but you have to. Life goes on."

"Why?"

Vicki heaved a sigh. "Get up and get moving."

Raina felt raw anger bubble up. "I'm not going! I can't."

"Yes, you can. You can't change what's happened. You can't bring him back from the dead. I know something about this personally."

She was talking about Justin, Raina's father, who'd died of a drug overdose without ever knowing that Vicki was pregnant with Raina.

She'd wondered if her mother had even mourned him. "I hurt!" Raina cried.

"We *all* hurt. But you're still alive and you have your senior year to finish and you have a network of people at the hospital asking when you'll be back and a ton of friends who love and care about you. It's time, Raina; pick up the pieces and go on."

"I hate you."

Vicki flinched, but she didn't back down. "Fine. Hate me. You're still getting out of that bed and going to school. I'm taking you, so start moving. Now."

twelve

HOLLY BECAME A minor celebrity at school. Classmates stepped aside for her in the halls, and teachers put no pressure on her in the classroom. Almost everybody looked at her with pitying eyes. She considered it ironic. There had been a time when she craved such deference. Now she felt like a freak in a sideshow. She heard the whispers. "That's her. The girl whose brother was murdered," and "I heard he got shot in the head—execution-style," and "How's she going to make it through?"

Friends other than Kathleen would look away when Holly came into a room. Or they'd get tears in their eyes. Even teachers teared up around her. Most people had known Hunter, so many felt personally connected to him. "They'll find something else to talk about soon enough," Kathleen assured her.

Strangely, Holly didn't truly care. Let them talk. It was a way to keep his memory alive. She felt oddly aloof, as if she were floating above the dramatics of her brother's death. She drove his old car to school, parked in the student lot and thought back to the time when she had so looked forward to driving it. Now that didn't matter either. Her parents hardly noticed her taking the car out of the driveway. And when she'd asked her dad for gas money, he'd reached into his pocket and handed over a twenty-dollar bill without comment.

She and Kathleen were the first to return to the hospital for their credit-earning hours with the Pink Angels. Sierra welcomed them both with hugs. "Will Raina be back?"

"I'm sure she will," Kathleen said. "Her mom wants her to finish high school, and this is one of the things she signed up for last year."

"I have your assignments." Sierra picked up a chart. "Holly, would you like to stay up on pediatrics?"

"If that's okay."

"And Kathleen, back to the gift shop and the medical library when they need you. Mrs. Nesbaum says she saved your Saturday job for you if you still want it."

Relieved, Kathleen said, "I'd like that."

It was obvious that Sierra was giving them the choicest spots.

"How about Raina?" Holly asked.

"I thought I'd start her in geriatrics, helping with the elderly—you know, transporting them to radiology, physical therapy, the OR. She's never done that before."

Holly guessed that the new learning curve would be good for Raina, while her own return to the children's floor would be equally good for her. She had an affinity for children, probably because she felt like a kid herself. At least, she used to feel that way. Over the past days she felt as if she'd grown old, skipping the growth process altogether. Facing the death of someone you loved must do that. She thought of her mother, still wandering the house like a lonely ghost. It frightened Holly. Bad enough to lose Hunter, but she felt she was losing her mother too.

Most evenings, Holly put some kind of dinner on the table, or her dad brought home takeout, mostly for the two of them. Evelyn lay alone in a darkened bedroom, nursing excruciating headaches—migraines, she said—escaping into one kind of pain in order to mask another.

"I don't feel like going to a party," Kathleen told Carson. He'd been telling her about a blowout planned for Halloween by one of his friends and urging her to come with him.

"Why? Do you think sitting around doing nothing is helping anybody?"

"It's disrespectful to Holly and Raina."

"You've been a good friend to them, but it's time to rejoin the land of the living."

Kathleen *wanted* to go with him; she was weary of feeling depressed, of being afraid of having too good a time, because Holly and Raina were still having trouble returning to the flow of high school life. Yet she didn't want to be disloyal.

Carson must have sensed her ambivalence; he put his arms around her and nuzzled her neck. "Come on, baby. If you look like you're having too much fun, we'll leave."

She gave him a sideway glance and suppressed a smile. "You won't overdo the beer, will you?" She remembered their last party and the mess that had come out of it.

"No way. Scout's honor."

His dark eyes danced with mischief. He could charm the scales off a fish. "Then we'll go."

The party house was decorated in a Halloween theme, with fake spiderwebs and ghosts made of sheets hanging from trees in the front yard. When they stepped onto the porch, a wild witch's cackle blared. Kathleen jumped, making Carson laugh. Inside, the living room furniture had been pushed against the walls and throngs of couples danced under synchronized blinking lights of every color. "There's a haunted house set up downstairs," Carson shouted above the racket. "Want to check it out?"

"Later." Kathleen looked around. She recognized many kids from other parties, yet still didn't

feel as if she fit in with Carson's bunch. She saw
Stephanie gyrating to the music between two
boys. Stephanie rubbed her body suggestively
against the boy in front, and he darted closer and
kissed her mouth. "I'm thirsty," Kathleen shouted
to Carson, turning away.

"This way." He took her hand and led her toward the back of the house and the kitchen, giving high fives to his friends along the way. A few
acknowledged Kathleen.

The kitchen was less crowded, but an ab-
solute mess. Cups, bottles, bags of chips and trays
of messy dips cluttered the counters. "Bombs
away," Kathleen said, surveying the debris.

"The maids will restore order tomorrow,"
Carson said, opening an ice chest.

His attitude irritated Kathleen. These kids
were rich and clueless about the real world,
where people worked to earn a living—Carson
included. They just assumed that someone was
always going to clean up their messes.

"How's this?" He offered her a Coke.

She reached around him and pulled out an
ice-cold wine cooler from the chest.

He looked startled. "Are you sure?"

"I'm not a child, Carson. I know how to
drink something besides soda pop."

"Rave on, Kathleen," he said. He stepped
over to the beer keg and drew himself a cup.

The wine cooler tasted sweet and cold and

went straight to Kathleen's head. For once, she didn't care. She was darn tired of keeping a lid on her emotions. She grabbed another bottle and ignored Carson's lifted eyebrow. "Let's dance."

She led the way back down the hall, and in seconds they were surrounded by the crush of bodies on the dance floor. She wasn't much of a dancer, but that hardly mattered. The music and lights, the noise, the drink and the warmth of bodies sent her into a zone of euphoria. Her blood tingled. She felt alive, free and wild, in sync with the universe. She didn't even care when Stephanie bumped her hard and sent her reeling.

"So sorry," Stephanie yelled. Her face was a blur to Kathleen, nothing but an impression of bright lipstick and mascara-smudged eyes.

Carson caught Kathleen and righted her. "Let's take a walk outside."

"I'm having fun! Isn't that wonderful?" She felt light-headed and giddy.

He steered her through the crowd to the door. She tripped a couple of times, but someone caught her and pushed her back toward Carson. The cool night air struck her face and she shivered. He got her to his car, and when he unlocked the door, she turned, threw her arms around his neck and kissed him long and deeply. Desire throbbed through her veins like hot water.

He had taught her how to kiss; she knew what he liked. Her clothes were confining and damp with perspiration. She wanted them off, wanted her skin next to his skin. Somehow she got the back door of the car open and pulled him inside and down on top of her. Everywhere his hands touched lit a fresh fire on her body.

She heard his voice in her ear. "You'd better stop right now, because I'm not going to be able to."

"Stop what? This?" She dragged his shirt out of his jeans and stroked his bare skin.

She heard his ragged breathing and reveled in the sheer power she possessed to make him groan, make him want her. The world began to spin. She felt dizzy, woozy. Carson was saying something, but she couldn't make out the words. For an instant, her whole body seemed to be floating. Then everything went black.

Holly's first date with Chad was a trick-or-treat party on the hospital's pediatric floor. She suggested it when he asked her out because she figured it would create the least amount of attitude from her parents. In actuality, they'd hardly asked any questions when she told them, which surprised her, since it was the first real date she'd ever had. The pediatric floor had been decorated for more than a week in the black and orange of

Halloween, and when Chad and Holly arrived at the recreation room at four, someone had set up tables and chairs and activity centers. The cafeteria had prepared a large sheet cake, and some clever person had set up drinks in IV bags and hung the bags on the familiar stainless steel poles. Holly laughed when she saw it, realizing that she, Raina and Kathleen might have thought up something like that in better days.

Chad seemed to know all the nurses, and they welcomed him with smiles and small talk. Holly watched him laugh and joke with them before commenting about it to him. He said, "I've been coming here on and off for treatment since I was three."

"That long?"

"Some years were better than others," he said with a self-conscious smile. "Last year I got a flu that I couldn't shake. It sent me here four times in six months."

"That's awful."

"Not so awful," he said. "It helped me meet you, didn't it?"

The way he looked at her when he said it sent a fluttering sensation to her stomach. "Hard way to meet girls," she mumbled, embarrassed by the fluttering. She shouldn't be feeling such things, not after what had happened to her brother, to her family.

The children who were mobile came to the

rec room. Four teens from the Pink Angels group showed up to help, and soon the room was rocking with squeals and laughter. Holly and Chad took bags of candy to the kids who couldn't make the trip down the hall. When they returned, the supervisory nurse announced, "We've arranged for wheelchairs to be brought up and for a few of you volunteers to take the older kids around to the nurses' stations on other floors." She passed out orange plastic pumpkin-shaped buckets and a list of the areas that were expecting the trick-or-treaters. "You'll end up in the cafeteria for another party. Just remember, everybody has to be back in their rooms by eight. Go have fun."

Much later, after all the patients had been tucked into their rooms, Chad walked Holly to her car in the mammoth parking garage. "Where are you parked?" she asked, unlocking the car door.

"Next level up." Before she could open the door, Chad caught her arm. "Wait. I—I want to ask you something."

She turned to face him and saw that his expression was anxious. She knew what he wanted before he even asked.

"Holly, I know that tonight was a trial run, but I want a serious date with you. A real one, where we go to the movies, maybe grab a burger."

She felt her hands getting clammy as nervousness took hold. Isn't this what she'd always wanted? For some guy to like her, ask her out? "I—I don't know."

He looked crestfallen. "It's the CF, isn't it?"

Certainly that was part of it for her, and she felt ashamed of feeling that way, but there *was* more to it. She didn't want to hurt Chad, but she didn't want to lie to him either. "I'm not sure I should be dating. It doesn't seem—" She hunted for a word. "It doesn't seem *right*, you know?"

"Because of your brother?"

Her eyes instantly filled with tears. "There are two Hollys inside me—happy Holly and sad Holly. Some days I get up, go to school, come here, forget about what's happened. And then when I'm getting into bed, I think, 'Gee, I haven't thought about Hunter all day.' And then it's like my mind hits a wall and I can't think about anything else. I can't tune out the loss of him and the hole left in our family." She stopped, realizing that she'd not been able to verbalize this to anyone, and now she was spilling everything to Chad, a near stranger. Embarrassed, she opened the car door and got inside. "I have to go."

He stepped back, his expression unreadable. "I'm not giving up, Holly. Not unless you tell me to get lost."

She couldn't tell him that.

He reached through the open window, touched her damp cheek. "I understand. My CF has let me see life through different eyes, and it's taught me things about people. About life. I'm *not* giving up on us."

She put the car in reverse and backed out of the space, leaving him alone in the shadows.

thirteen

FROM THE MOMENT Kathleen opened her eyes, she wished she hadn't. Light poured through her bedroom window, stabbing into her eyeballs like daggers. Her head hurt and her lips felt glued together. She moaned and put her pillow over her face, wishing the daylight away. Slowly, images of the night before came back to her. She recalled blinking lights, driving music, the cool interior of Carson's car and his hot breath on her throat and . . . nothing else.

She peeked out at her bedside clock radio. Eleven o'clock. She'd slept far into Sunday morning, and she wondered why her mother had let her. She staggered to the bathroom, splashed cold water on her face, looked at herself in the mirror and made another moaning sound. She was wearing her green sleeping T-shirt emblazoned with SNOW WHITE LIVES!, with no memory of having put it on.

She knew she had to go out and face her

mother. What would she say? A wave of nausea hit her and she returned to bed just as her cell phone chirped. She saw Carson's number and thought about not answering it, but then realized he might be able to fill in the blank spaces in her memory.

"You're alive?" he said when she answered.

"Barely."

He chuckled.

"How many of those coolers did I drink?"

"One too many."

She saw nothing humorous in her situation. "Um—how did I get home, and in my bed?"

"I brought you in. And I did it without waking your mother too. You owe me, babe."

"My clothes—"

"I'm innocent. I poured you into bed, pulled up the covers and left. Honest."

Maybe she'd gotten up and changed and just didn't remember. "Are we still friends?"

He laughed suggestively. "Very close friends."

An image of herself pawing his body flashed and she sat straight up. Her head pounded. "Did we—I mean—how close are we?"

"Are you asking me if we're now 'friends with benefits'?"

His use of the familiar term so embarrassed her that she felt hot, then cold all over. She squeezed the cell phone. "Please tell me."

He waited a few torturous beats. "Believe it or not, I prefer my girls to be alert, aware and in full control of their senses when things get hot between us."

Relief rushed through her. "So I'm still—?" She couldn't get the word out.

"You're still the one I want more than anybody."

"Really?"

"From the first day we met."

"Oh, Carson! I'm so sorry about last night. I—I didn't mean to—to go crazy that way. I've just been sad for so long and I wanted to be happy again. Forgive me?"

"Nothing to forgive. It was nice to see your wild side. And there was another fringe benefit."

"What was that?"

"I left the party stone cold sober."

As it turned out, Kathleen didn't have to tell her mother anything about the night before, because when she ventured out of her room, Mary Ellen wasn't home. She'd left a note on the counter saying that she'd gone off to church and lunch with Stewart, the man she was seeing from the multiple sclerosis support group. *Fine*, Kathleen thought, surprised by her resentment. Had Mary Ellen even checked on her before she left?

Kathleen drank some juice, took a long, hot shower and called Holly. "How did the hospital party go last night? And your date with Chad?" she added, suddenly remembering.

"The party was fun. The kids had a great time. Chad and I worked, so we didn't have much alone time."

This didn't sound like Holly, who was prone to babble on when it came to a guy she liked. "So, you want to do something this afternoon? A movie? I can check what's playing and the start times—" Kathleen stopped herself. She'd forgotten it was Sunday and that Holly's family had "together time" on Sundays.

"That would be all right," Holly said.

"You sure?"

"Mom's taking a nap and Dad's out working in the garage."

"Oh. But it's all right for you to take off?"

"Perfectly," Holly said, with a flatness in her voice. "No one seems to care much anymore."

"That can't be true. I've lived with you. I know how much they care."

Holly didn't say anything right away. "Yes, they care. They just care differently now. Everything's different now."

"Your birthday's coming up, Raina. What would you like?"

Vicki's question gave Raina pause. Raina was curled up on the sofa, under an old quilt, mindlessly surfing TV channels. Outside, a chilly

November rain was falling, pelting the windows like tears. In one week she would be eighteen, on Thanksgiving Day. "I haven't thought about it."

"Think about it."

"Nothing comes to mind."

"A shopping spree? A trip to Orlando for a few of the attractions? You could take Kathleen and Holly—my treat."

"I don't care."

Vicki walked over and turned off the television. "Raina, please talk to me. You've got to snap out of this funk."

"Snap *out* of it?" Raina was incredulous. "My boyfriend was murdered! How do I snap out of that?"

Vicki looked weary. "I'm sorry. That was a poor choice of words. I just want to see my daughter again . . . the one I used to have fun with, who used to talk to me about everything." Vicki sat on the edge of the coffee table and faced Raina. "Your grades are abysmal. You rarely go anywhere with your friends. You're turning eighteen in a week and you don't even want a present. I don't know what to do to help you."

"Nothing," Raina said. She felt dead inside, like a plant left too long without water. "I just have to work through it on my own."

"What about college? You used to talk about going to college."

"Mom, everything I ever wanted was wrapped

up in Hunter. I was going to find a college near him in Indiana. He held all of me in his hands. *All* of me."

"How about nursing? You wanted to be a nurse. At the hospital, they raved to me about you in the Pink Angels program."

"I like the hospital. They put me on the floor with the old people, you know."

"I can ask them to move you to an area you'd like better."

"Why? One place is as good as any. Some of the old patients are cranky. Some are really nice. But do you know what I think about when I'm with them?" She didn't want an answer, so she said, "I think about how Hunter will never get to grow old. He barely had time to grow up."

"You *will* love again, Raina," Vicki insisted after a long silence.

"Really? *You* never did."

Vicki recoiled. "I never took time for it. I had a child to raise and a job to do. Love just wasn't on my dance card. I have no regrets."

Raina held her mother's gaze. "Then we have something in common. I don't ever want to be in love again either."

She stood, wrapped the quilt tightly around herself and went up to her room. A night-light glowed from a wall socket as the rain fell relentlessly outside. The glimmer of light reflected off the glass angel Hunter had given her the year before. "To watch over you," he'd said. Last year, getting back together with him had made her birthday the happiest ever. This year, it would be her saddest. She cradled the figurine in her hands, pressed it against her cheek, longing to feel Hunter touch her, hear his voice say her name. There were only the sound of the rain and the feel of the cool, hard glass on her skin.

"We've got to do something special for Raina's birthday," Kathleen told Carson. They were watching a movie in his home theater, but she wasn't paying it much attention.

"*We* do?"

"Normally I'd ask Holly, but I can't very well do that now, can I?"

Carson paused the movie with the remote. "Point taken. What did you have in mind?"

"If I knew, I wouldn't be picking your brain, would I?"

"Let's see, I could take the three of you to a hotel—"

She slugged his shoulder. "Be serious."

"Do I not look serious?"

She started to stand, but he hauled her onto his lap. "All kidding is over. Do you have any ideas?"

"It has to be something fun, something neither she nor Holly has ever done before. Something memorable." She nibbled on a fingernail. "And something that doesn't cost a lot of money. I don't have too much saved up, and Christmas is coming."

"Sounds like you need a fairy godmother to show up."

"I don't know how to help my two best friends," she said softly. "They hurt so bad, and I don't know how to help them."

"Still no word about Hunter's shooter?"

"Nothing." Kathleen picked at a button on the front of his shirt. "People die every day in Tampa. You never think about that until it happens to someone you know. How do you fill up the hole that's left?"

"Maybe you have to dig another hole," he said. "What do you say we plan something really low-key? No party. No crowds."

She considered his suggestion. "Sounds like an *un*birthday."

"Leave it to me," he said.

"To you?"

"Trust me."

Through his mother's connections, Carson arranged a supper for the three friends in the planetarium under a glass-domed ceiling. A waiter from the country club, dressed in a white coat, served them at a table draped with pale blue linen and adorned with bone china, crystal, silver and a centerpiece of fresh white roses—choices Teresa made, she said, "because beauty has a way of dulling grief."

While they ate, classical music played softly, and on one wall an enormous movie screen showed amazing photos of galaxies thousands of light-years away taken by the Hubble telescope. The star masses looked like explosions of flowers, in every color imaginable, strewn on a blanket of black. Overhead, real stars glittered in the dark sky above the dome.

The waiter handed Raina a card that read "Happy 18th, Raina, from . . . Your Angels." He gave Holly a card, also signed "Your Angels."

"This is very wonderful," Raina said, looking at her friends. "Thanks."

"Kathleen's doing," Holly said.

"I had some help from a guy with a vivid imagination."

"Lucky you," Raina said sincerely.

Kathleen beamed inwardly. Carson had done something extraordinary and touched all their hearts with his magic. And she knew that no matter what the future held for her and Carson, she would forever remember the night he gave her the universe.

fourteen

"WHAT DO YOU mean we're going away for Christmas?" Holly stared at her father, hardly believing what he'd just told her. They were sitting at the kitchen table eating cereal for supper because Evelyn was in bed with a headache.

"I just think it's the best thing for us this year."

"But we always have Christmas at home. If Mom doesn't feel like decorating, we can do it together."

He shook his head. "No, we can't."

"I can do it by myself, then." She knew exactly where the Christmas boxes were stashed in the attic. "I'll put it all away too, after Christmas is over."

He touched her hand. "Honey, it has nothing to do with the work. I really don't think your mother can stand to see all those decorations—all the stuff you and your brother made for our trees when you were kids. She's not up to it. And I'm not sure I am either."

Dismayed, Holly sorted mentally through the

collection of old ornaments. She and Hunter used to have contests to see which of them could make the prettiest or the most unusual items for the family Christmas tree. And Evelyn had supervised so much of the crafting—stained-glass baubles made with specially colored sand baked in the oven, felt reindeer and wreaths, glitter-covered stars and angels—every item held a memory. And naturally, there was the crèche. They had worked on that as a family over the years, sanding bisqueware, painstakingly painting the pieces and taking them to be kiln-fired, turning them into the Holy Family, shepherds, wise men, angels and a barnyard full of animals. It was Hunter and Holly's job to set up the crèche every year on the credenza in the family room. They usually dressed the surface with angel hair, a few fake palm trees and a wooden cutout of a stable and manger Hunter had made. It had been a family tradition, and now it was being taken away.

"Where will we go?" Holly asked.

Her father brightened. "A ski lodge in upper New Hampshire. I checked it out on the Web and had the place send brochures. I'll show them to you."

"We don't ski."

"It doesn't matter. It'll be a real change for us. Don't you think a white Christmas would be fun?"

"Tons," she said without expression.

"I'll get the brochures. The place is really

nice. You'll see." He stood, but she caught the sleeve of his shirt.

"Dad, is Mom going to be okay?"

He looked down at her, his expression switching from eager-happy mode to confused sadness. "I hope so, baby. She just needs some time."

Holly's heart thudded. There was so much she wanted to say to her dad, so many questions she wanted to ask. Their world had turned savage and dark, and now all the things she had been taught to believe in seemed fanciful and shallow. As she looked up at him, at the tired lines in his face, her throat closed up. She let go of his sleeve. "It'll be fun to see snow," she said, because she knew he needed to hear it.

"Maybe your dad's right, though. Getting away might be good for your family," Kathleen said.

Holly had gone to Kathleen's to tell her the news. School was out for the holidays, and without the usual Christmas preparations, Holly had nothing to do except pack a suitcase. It didn't help that Kathleen's house was gaily decorated.

"I guess," Holly said. "Sometimes I think things will never be normal again."

"What's 'normal' anyway?"

"They don't even gripe at me anymore. I feel invisible."

"What about you and Chad? How's that going?" Kathleen changed the subject.

"We've gone to a couple of movies together."

"Want to double with me and Carson over the break?"

"We won't be back until New Year's Day, then it's back to school."

"We can still double sometime."

"I'm not sure I want to date Chad."

"Why? I thought you liked him."

"I do. But I feel sorry for him too." Holly picked at the fringe on a Christmas pillow beside her on the sofa. "I'm not sure I want to get mixed up with a guy who is probably going to die before long."

Kathleen looked startled. "You don't know if that's going to happen to Chad. Some CF patients live a long time, what with all the new drugs and stuff."

"Like I want to wait around for the other shoe to drop. Why start caring for him in the first place? Where's the smarts in that?"

Kathleen said nothing, so Holly assumed she'd gotten her point. Across the room, the lights of Kathleen's tree twinkled. Holly had never felt less like facing Christmas. Maybe she'd take a page from her mother's life and sleep through the holidays. She cleared her throat. "The ski lodge is pretty in the pictures. Maybe I'll make a snowman and date him."

Kathleen giggled. "Look at your nails. They're a mess. You can't go to a ski lodge with ugly nails."

Holly looked down at her chipped nails, some bitten down to the quick. She had started painting her nails so that she would stop biting them. She didn't even remember when she'd started biting them again. "I'll paint them later."

"No, we'll give each other manicures." Kathleen jumped up. "Wait here, I'll go gather my stuff."

"But I don't—" Holly was protesting to the air, because Kathleen was gone. She sighed, and was staring at the tree, feeling sad, when she heard the mechanical swish of Mary Ellen's wheelchair. She looked up and saw Kathleen's mother emerge from the doorway.

"Hello," Holly said, forcing a smile.

"Hi, honey." Mary Ellen stopped next to the sofa. "I didn't mean to eavesdrop, but I heard you say you were going away for the holidays."

"Dad's idea."

"I feel so bad for you and your family, Holly." Mary Ellen looked as if she had more to say, so Holly waited patiently. "I know a little myself about losing someone you love."

"Your husband."

Mary Ellen nodded. "I just wanted to crawl into a corner and die. In fact, I couldn't understand why he'd died and I'd lived. I certainly didn't want to face my life without him. I didn't want to face advancing MS without him either."

Holly was well aware of how Mary Ellen's MS had affected Kathleen. "Nothing's ever going to be the same at home."

"That's true. But things will get better."

Holly wanted to believe her.

"In the end it was my child who saved me from myself. She was only eight, you know. Just a scared little girl. My turning point came when I was lying in my hospital bed wishing I could die and I looked out the ICU window. I saw her standing there, nose pressed against the glass, her red hair all wild. And I thought, 'Someone had better brush that child's hair before it snarls into a thousand knots.' "

Mary Ellen chuckled at the memory. "It was the first positive thought I'd had in weeks. The first time I'd thought about someone other than myself. And I realized that my little girl needed me. She was mine and Jim's. And I needed her. Not because of my MS, but because she was all I had left of him."

Holly had never appreciated what Kathleen's mother had gone through. It was different from her losing Hunter, but it was also the same. "I'm the one who's left, all that's made up of my mom and dad." She hadn't considered that before.

"You are. It is a large responsibility to be the one left standing. Your parents are devastated, and it may seem like you've fallen through the cracks, but they love and appreciate you even though it might not seem so just now."

Holly wasn't sure she was ready to shoulder all their expectations. "Does it . . . your heart . . . ever stop hurting?"

"Yes and no. You never forget, but you do see 'happy' again. You don't think you will, but you do."

Holly nodded as a lump of emotion rose in her throat. "Sometimes it seems like that man murdered my whole family."

Mary Ellen reached over and squeezed Holly's hand. "Don't let him win." After a few emotionally charged moments, she put her chair into reverse and turned for the doorway. "One more thought before your manicurist returns. Don't be afraid to care about someone just because he may not be facing the brightest of futures."

Chad.

"If the good Lord had told me when I was your age that I was going to be sick and that my husband was going to die in a car wreck, I still would have chosen the life that I have. I loved Jim with all my heart. And he gave me Kathleen. It's been enough."

Raina thought the Christmas holidays would never end. She spent every minute she could at the hospital, haunting the corridors like a ghost, volunteering for the most menial tasks to stay busy. The great tree in the lobby had been decorated entirely with white paper doves and tiny white lights. Resident doctors could be seen wearing Santa caps, and the windows in the newborns' nurseries were encircled with tinsel and colored lights. Everybody seemed filled with the Christmas spirit. Except for Raina.

Every Christmas song weighed on her heart. Building snowmen in meadows seemed stupid, and she didn't care if Santa Claus came to town, or if Frosty turned into a puddle. Nothing mattered, because nothing was the same as when Hunter had been alive.

Her mother dragged her shopping, bullied her into helping to decorate the town house, demanded she help with baking. Two days before Christmas, Raina began to notice that Vicki was storing up more than the usual pile of cookies in tins. She was baking bread and Christmas cakes, pies and puff pastries. Raina grumbled, "We'll never eat all this food."

"I know. I'm just in the mood to cook. We'll freeze what we don't eat, have Christmas all year long."

"No thanks."

"We can't just skip Christmas," Vicki said, taking a roast out of the oven.

"Knock yourself out."

"I'd appreciate some enthusiasm. And some help. Decorate these cookies for me."

Raina stared at the doughy lumps next in line for the oven. Jars of colored sugar and candy bells, hearts and sprinkles were lined up on the table.

"Please," Vicki said.

Raina tackled the job halfheartedly.

Vicki turned on some Christmas CDs and began humming along. Raina wanted to scream. She also began to notice that her mother kept glancing at the clock, casually, but often. Raina ignored the cheeriness, shook red and green sugar crystals onto some raw dough, smashed a few candy silver balls onto the surface and considered it a very ugly wreath. She was finishing up the tray when the doorbell rang.

"Will you get that?" Vicki asked. "I'm covered in flour."

She wasn't, but Raina went to the front door anyway. She opened it and stared in shocked silence at the young woman standing on the doormat. "Emma."

"Merry Christmas, Raina."

Behind Emma, Raina saw Jon-Paul, who waved and grinned.

Raina began to tremble all over, and emotion clogged her throat. Emma opened her arms and Raina dissolved into her sister's embrace.

fifteen

HOLLY THOUGHT THAT snow was highly over-rated. Yes, it looked pretty from a distance, but up close, once people had stepped in it and smushed it, car tires had rolled over it and salt had eroded it, snow wasn't very pretty at all. The rooms at the lodge were rustic-looking, with pine walls and oversized furniture covered in wool and leather. Mike Harrison had reserved a suite for his family, so Holly had her own room, a tiny space all to herself. A large common area sepa-rated her room from her parents'. The bigger room held a sofa, squishy chairs, a kitchenette, a large television and shelves full of old books. A wall of glass looked out onto a private balcony, and beyond the snow-covered slopes and grounds of the resort, the mountains of New Hampshire rose like sleeping giants.

The lodge's great room, below their floor, was awash with people in colorful ski clothes, hun-kered around the biggest fireplace Holly had ever seen. Adjoining the great room was a large dining room, where meals were served family-style at long wooden tables decorated with candles and fir branches laced with red ribbon. A magnificent Christmas tree draped in lights, red bows and moose-shaped ornaments filled up one corner. A toy train circled the tree's base endlessly, tirelessly, waiting for Christmas to arrive.

Secretly, Holly was shocked by the number of people who had left their homes and come to a lodge to celebrate Christmas. How many of them were running away from memories? They all looked so happy. When she and her parents sat in the dining room amid the strangers, or around the fireplace or with the skiers on the beginners' slope, she wondered if anyone could see into the dark places inside the Harrison family. Or did the whiteness of the snow make everything and everyone look pure and clean?

Her father turned into a tour director, planning every minute of the days, her mother stoic, going along with all his suggestions. They drank bottomless cups of hot chocolate, played video games and shot billiards in a huge game room, sank into hot tubs and swam in a heated pool every evening. Holly skied on rented equipment after a few lessons on the bunny trails, alongside her mother. Neither of them was very good, and Holly's face felt frozen afterward.

Their happy family vacation fell apart on Christmas Eve. In their suite, Mike said, "There's a little church in town having services at seven and eleven. The sanctuary looks like a picture postcard. You'll love it. We can go to the late service, sing some Christmas hymns, light some candles."

"I don't want to go to church," Evelyn said. She was on the sofa, flipping through a magazine.

"Honey, it's Christmas Eve. We always attend church."

"At home," Evelyn said. "We're not at home."

"I'll go, Dad," Holly said, sensing a storm brewing between her parents.

"Take Holly."

"We're a family. We go together."

"Really?" Evelyn tossed the magazine on the coffee table. "I'm on vacation. I don't want to go."

Silence fell. Holly saw frustration etched into her father's face. "Um—we could open presents after," she interjected. They had brought their wrapped gifts in large plastic containers. "Then we could sleep in tomorrow. Until lunchtime if we want."

"Why should I go?" Evelyn asked, as if Holly hadn't spoken. "What have we got to celebrate, Michael? What has God done for us this year? What have we got to say thank you for? I haven't got anything to be grateful for. Have you?"

"Don't blame God for what happened."

"Who should I blame? Tell me. Who?"

"God loves—"

"Don't." Evelyn got up and walked into the bedroom, slamming the door behind her.

Mike Harrison stared at the closed door. Minutes later, he grabbed his coat. "I need some fresh air," he told Holly.

And then Holly was alone in front of the wall of frigid windows. She shivered. The room had gone cold. As cold as death. Outside, snow began to fall.

It took several hours for welcomes to be exchanged, dinner to be served and eaten, Vicki to slip away to her room and Jon-Paul to settle in front of the TV, but eventually, Raina was sitting in her bedroom, alone with Emma. The conversation at dinner had been chatty and full of updates about Emma's life.

Yes, she was doing well enough with the transplant to have cut back on her antirejection medications.

Yes, she loved being married.

Yes, she had gotten a part-time job after decorating her and Jon-Paul's condo twice.

Yes, her mom and dad were fine.

Emma's first question to Raina was "How are you doing?"

"Not too good. But I guess you know that already."

"When your mom called, she sounded at her wits' end."

Raina thought it strange to hear Emma refer to Vicki as *her* mom, when she had given birth to both of them, but her sister apparently didn't feel any special kinship with her biological mother. Did Emma wonder about her father?

Raina cleared her throat. "I know she's worried about me. I try, but I just can't get on top of this thing."

"You've suffered a horrible trauma. It's all right to be sad."

Raina's eyes welled with tears. "See what I mean? Just talking about it even a tiny bit makes me fall to pieces." Emma handed Raina a tissue from a nearby box. "You and Jon-Paul should buy stock in this stuff. I go through it by the crate."

Emma laughed softly. "I didn't know your Hunter well, but I remember how the two of you looked at each other. That's what sticks with me. I know you loved each other."

Raina blew her nose. "We did. Even Mom understood that."

"She loves you too."

"We've had our problems."

"All teenage girls have problems with their mothers."

"Did you?"

"I was sick, so I didn't reject her very often. Truthfully, I was angry at my biological mother—

the one who had passed along the lousy DNA. There is a genetic link with cancer, you know."

Raina knew that from her work at the hospital and with the Pink Angels. "Maybe it was from your father's side," she ventured.

"You mean *our* father's side, don't you?"

"You know about him?"

"Vicki told me everything."

"And you're not mad about it?"

"Why should I be? He was only a sperm donor. Carl raised me. He's my daddy."

Raina was taken aback, somehow disappointed that Emma didn't have a stronger reaction to Vicki's deception.

"Listen," Emma said, leaning closer, "not all adopted kids are burning to know who they came from. Growing up, I had three adopted friends, and only one wanted to find her birth parents. I never did. Believe me, though, it came up when my doctors started talking about a bone marrow transplant. But even then, I wasn't eager to go through the ordeal of the search. Plus a part of me thought I was being disloyal to the mom and dad who raised me."

"But your life was at stake."

"I didn't say it was rational." Emma smiled again. "But it worked out all right, didn't it? I signed up with the registry and so did you. We were meant to find each other."

Raina thought about it. "Didn't you ever

wonder if you had a brother or sister some-where?"

Emma was silent, and Raina knew she was trying to formulate an answer that wouldn't hurt Raina's feelings. "I never minded being an only child. I was the princess in my family. I had good friends . . . a few who had knock-down, drag-out fights with their siblings, and I always felt grateful that I didn't have to share anything. Then there was the leukemia—that colored everything." She looked sheepish. "Once I stopped being a selfish little brat, my world got a whole lot larger."

Raina understood. "I'll admit that I didn't mind having Mom all to myself when I was younger. But when I found out about you, I was, well, *mad*! I felt like she'd lied to me for my whole life. We were best friends. And friends don't lie to each other."

"She told me she was sorry that she didn't tell you sooner, that it had been a mistake to keep it a secret for so long," Emma said. "I don't think she was prepared for how much the truth was going to affect you."

Raina rotated her shoulders, sore from ten-sion. If Emma didn't care, why should she? "She says there are no more secrets. I hope that's true. What matters to me is that we found each other. I'm glad I have a sister. I'm glad you came for a visit. How long can you stay?"

"We leave on the twenty-eighth. Jon-Paul

has to go back to work and we have to make up Christmas with our families."

For the first time, Raina considered the Delaschmidts and Jon-Paul's family. Of course they would want to have holiday time with Emma and Jon-Paul too. "Tell them thank you for sharing."

Emma looked deep into Raina's eyes. "You're my sister. You gave me the marrow from your bones and saved my life. It was a most precious gift, Raina. Without it, I would certainly be dead by now."

Raina's eyes filled. "You deserve to be happy."

"And so do you."

Emma reached out and tucked a long strand of Raina's hair behind her ear, and Raina's tears spilled down her cheeks. "Hunter used to do that same thing," she whispered. "The only time I'm happy is when I sleep and dream of him. I see him in my dreams and I feel overjoyed. I want him back so much."

"Yikes! Did everybody decide to return their Christmas gifts at the mall today?" Kathleen was in the car with Carson, and they were on their second cruise of the mall parking lot looking for a space. "Are you sure you want to exchange that game?"

"I wanted to get out of the house," Carson said. "A guy can take just so much family to-getherness."

"I think your great-grandmother is sweet."

"And so are my two aunts, two uncles, three cousins and their little dog, Toto." His mother's family from Miami had descended on them for the holidays, turning their normally tranquil home into a madhouse. He swerved to miss a car backing out, shoved his car into reverse and pulled into the space.

"There *are* a lot of relatives hanging around. But your mom seems really happy to be with them." Kathleen had missed most of the conversations because everyone was speaking Spanish, but they all had been nice to her, offering smiles along with platters of rich food. Carson's ninety-two-year-old *bisabuela*, great-grandmother, kept touching Kathleen's red hair and declaring it *muy bonito*—very pretty.

Kathleen and Carson walked into the crowded mall hand in hand. The day was sunny and the temperature was almost eighty degrees. Kathleen wondered how Holly was faring in the New Hampshire snow. The sudden appearance of Emma was keeping Raina occupied, which was a good thing.

"Everyone will be gone by New Year's Eve. Of course, school starts the second of January." Carson didn't sound too happy about that, but she knew he'd been studying hard and his grades were up.

"Any more flak from your dad about your becoming an EMT?"

"I start at the community college in late August, but on academic probation. He says if I do well, he'll approve my EMT plans. Although I suspect he thinks I'll love college courses so much that I'll want to switch to a four-year program at the university of his choice."

"Don't be crabby. I'll be at USF—"

Someone called Carson's name and they both turned to see Stephanie descending the escalator. "My favorite person," Kathleen muttered under her breath.

"Don't be crabby," Carson whispered with a sly grin.

Stephanie glided through the crowd, leaving a trail of gawkers in her wake. Naturally, she looked stunning in a microskirt and stylish sandals, her long dark hair flowing behind her. "Carson! How are you?" She came up, leaned close and kissed both his cheeks, a common custom, Kathleen had learned, among Spaniards, Cubans and, apparently, South Americans.

"Fine, Steffie," Carson said. "How was Christmas?"

"Rio was rocking." She shook her finger at him. "You should have visited like I asked. Mama wanted to see you again."

Stephanie had invited him to Rio de Janeiro

for the holidays? This was the first Kathleen had heard about it.

"Not possible. My house is thick with relatives," he said.

Stephanie looked delighted. "*Bisabuela* is here? I'm coming over tonight. I *love* her."

Kathleen's mouth almost dropped open. Where did this girl get off inviting herself this way?

For the first time, Stephanie glanced at Kathleen. "I mean, unless you have other plans."

"No plans," Kathleen said sweetly. She wasn't about to get into a turf war over Carson's great-grandmother!

"Then I'll see you later. You can fill me in on what's been happening since I've been out of the country." Stephanie made a production of looking at her watch. "Must run. A spring fashion show starts down at Burdines in fifteen. Come watch me walk the runway—third floor." She breezed away.

Carson sagged visibly. "Why didn't you tell her we had plans?"

"And deprive you of the joy of her company? Wouldn't think of it."

He scowled. "Her eyes looked too bright," he said, becoming serious.

"I didn't notice."

"I think she's high."

His assessment sobered Kathleen instantly. "She had on a lot of makeup for the show."

"It wasn't makeup. I've seen that look in her eyes before."

"What are you going to do about it?"

"There's nothing I can do. I'm not getting sucked into that black hole again." He tucked his arm around Kathleen. "Come on. Let's get this game exchanged and get out of here."

sixteen

THE FIRST WEEK of January, Holly went to Tarpon Springs with Chad and attended the Epiphany service with him and his family. They were members of the Greek Orthodox Church, which meant their church calendar was different from Holly's and they celebrated Christmas two weeks after December 25. Holly had never stepped inside such a magnificent church. Built in the shape of a cross and elaborately decorated in the Byzantine tradition, the church looked exotic and mysterious, like something from a history book. Gold sparkled from every wall, the ceiling, the altar area. Beautifully painted panels called icons, depicting the Madonna and Christ, adorned the entranceway. The priest wore an elaborate bejeweled gown and headdress. Candles glowed and incense burned, filling the sanctuary with a sweet, smoky aroma. The music sounded medieval, totally unlike the hymns she knew. She was mesmerized.

Afterward, Chad took her to his home, a small white stucco house in a neighborhood near the bay, where he lived with his parents and three younger brothers: Timothy, twelve, and twins Jonathan and Stephano, seven. Sumptuous cooking smells floated through the rooms, many as exotic to her as the church service. Chad's grandparents came for dinner, as did an aunt and uncle and their family of four. The house brimmed with talk, laughter, Greek music, good food and squealing children. Holly sat demurely on the sidelines, mostly watching, answering questions when asked and envying the robust family life spilling out in front of her.

Her house had once been a gathering place too, with her family hosting cookouts and potluck suppers, dessert fests after youth group meetings and Christmas caroling. But months had passed since her parents had opened their doors for such an event. She missed the gatherings.

When the meal had been eaten and the table cleared, Chad leaned over and whispered, "Want to go someplace with me?"

He took her to the harbor, where sturdy-looking fishing boats were anchored and gulls circled overhead, flinging cries at the blue sky. They walked to a marina, to sleek moored sailboats. Chad stopped in front of one boat painted white, with weathered teak railings. It looked older than most of the others, and only big enough for maybe four people.

"Yours?" she asked.

"Meet *Katalina*, my first true love. I've had her for years." He helped Holly on board, handed her a life jacket.

"I can swim," she said.

"It's the rule. Put it on." He untied the line holding the boat in its berth and cast off. He sat in the stern and cranked a tiny outboard motor. "This will get us out to open water."

Holly breathed in the salt air, watched the water turn from pale green to deep blue. Beyond the shelter of the bay, the gulf stretched endlessly, seeming to kiss the sky at the horizon. Once in open water, Chad cut the noisy motor. He untied the rigging and hoisted the mainsail, watching it fill with wind. He took the tiller and the boat began to skim across the water like a bird coasting on air.

"You never told me you sailed," she said, astounded by his expertise.

"I'm Greek. It's in our blood." His smile was shot with sunlight. "Have you sailed before?"

"Never. But I could get used to it. This is great!" She turned her face skyward, let the wind rush over her skin and the sun warm her.

"Want to take command? Just keep her nose to the wind and her sail full."

Holly moved cautiously to the stern, took the tiller and held the boat steady.

"You're a natural," he shouted after a few minutes.

She smiled, feeling an exhilaration that made her light-headed.

He taught her how to tack, come about, duck when the boom swung around. He took over only once, when, for a heart-stopping moment, the boat leaned far to one side and threatened to capsize.

In the golden sun-drenched afternoon, Holly lost track of time, and only when red streaked the sky did the wind slack and a calm settle in. Water lapped the sides of the boat. Holly felt it gently rock and watched the shoreline far away, not certain she wanted to return.

Chad scooted closer to her, put his arm around her. "The motor will get us in when we're ready. Let's watch the sunset."

She leaned against him, felt his sun-warmed body and closed her eyes. "I've had a really good time."

"Good. I'm glad it was with me." He stroked her hair. "Not to ruin the moment, but what did you think of my crazy family?"

"I liked them."

"I apologize for the twins."

She remembered how they had whispered

and giggled every time she glanced their way. "They're cute."

"You're a novelty—I've never brought a girl home before."

"How about sailing?"

"You're first again. Between the homeschooling and the CF, *Katalina* has been my best friend for years."

It touched her that he had been alone so much. "She's a good friend to have."

"What did you think of our church?"

"It was different from what I'm used to. It's beautiful, though."

"The first time I went into a Protestant church, I thought the friend who took me was playing a joke," he said with a laugh. "Everything was so plain."

Above, the red and gold sky was turning indigo, dark and inky. "With so many different houses to choose from, how does God pick which one to live in?" she mused.

"Perhaps he chooses many."

"You think he's fickle? Because I do. Actually, I'm not sure I believe in him anymore."

There! She'd said it. The thing that had been on her mind since the day they'd buried her brother. She turned to look at Chad's face, growing dim in the failing light, to see if she'd shocked him. "You think I'm terrible, don't you?" she said.

"All my life I've believed in God, and now I don't."

"I could never think you're terrible, Holly." His arm tightened around her. "I've wondered the same thing myself every time I've gone to the hospital. Why did *I* get sick? Why do *I* have CF? No one asked me if I wanted it. I was just born with it."

She instantly grasped the inequity, the injustice of what had happened to him. She felt a rising anger toward the Being who supposedly controlled all things and could have prevented Chad's illness and Hunter's death. "My dad says it's a mystery, which is another way to say 'Who knows?' What a cop-out."

"My mom says she's got a lot to ask God about when she sees him." Chad grinned. "Even God had better duck when an angry Greek mother approaches."

All Holly could think was that her own mother, a woman who had revered God all her life, was finished with him. And now, so was Holly.

With the failing sun, the evening had turned colder. She heard Chad's breath wheeze in her ear and realized that the night air wasn't doing him any good.

He said, "I have a windbreaker stashed under the front bench."

"You should wear it," she said, suddenly concerned about him.

He ignored her. He pulled the starter and the little motor kicked to life. They made it back to the pier with neither of them wearing the windbreaker. His father was waiting for them at the berth, pacing, his expression dark and serious. "Where have you been? Your mother is worried."

"We got to talking. The sun dropped before we realized it."

"You know you have no lights! You could have capsized."

"We're fine." Chad helped Holly from the boat. He was wheezing hard, forcing words through blue-tinged lips. His father took his arm, but Chad shook him off.

Holly knew instinctively that Chad felt humiliated, but there was nothing she could do to help.

"I will take you home," his father said sternly, "and then I will drive Holly to her house."

"Dad!"

"This is not a suggestion!" his father roared.

Holly identified with Chad's embarrassment. She vowed to send him an e-mail the minute she got home, assuring him that she understood, that he'd treated her to an amazing day she would never forget, and that she wanted to see him again as soon as he felt better. And yet, although she wouldn't tell him so, she had also found his father's outburst oddly comforting. Her father used to bellow at her in the same tone, using almost the same words, in the days when he had supervised her every movement. Before Hunter died. Before God abandoned them.

Emma's visit did Raina a world of good, although Raina wasn't sure why—nothing had changed in her life. Perhaps it was the connectedness she had felt knowing that their DNA ran together like a stream. Raina had always loved her friends, but having a sister was different. And even though they had no shared history, Raina liked knowing there was someone whose facial features mirrored hers, someone who had her mannerisms, who even sounded a little like her. It helped her see Holly's loss of Hunter in a whole new light.

In February, she went to Holly. "I need your help."

"My help?" Raina's request surprised Holly because Raina had been living in another world for months. "Well, sure. What do you want?"

They were sitting together in the hospital cafeteria on a Saturday, nibbling on lunch. Being a Pink Angel gave Raina something else to do on Saturdays besides sit at home and feel lonely. Holly had told her that she came for the same reasons. Why else volunteer for no credit and no pay? At least Kathleen was paid for working most Saturdays.

"If I don't get my grades up, I'm not going to graduate. My counselor called me in on Friday and delivered the bad news."

"You're kidding!"

"Does this look like the face of a kidder?"

Holly shook her head. "How can I help?"

"Study with me. *Make* me crack the books. I really don't want to be stuck in summer school, or worse, have to take the equivalency test to get my diploma." They'd used to study in the library together all the time. Before the world fell apart. "You still study, don't you?"

Holly reddened. "It keeps my mind busy."

"Sorry. I didn't mean to sound sarcastic." Raina took a breath. "You're smart, Holly. The smartest of all of us. I'm jealous because I can't get my act together."

Raina's smile looked watery, but Holly understood. "The books are a retreat for me. A place to hide when my brain gets full of stuff I can't dump . . . stuff I don't want to think about, or remember."

"I guess we all have our hiding places."

Dishes and glassware clanked as the cafeteria filled with lunchtime personnel. "So, how are you doing with the new boyfriend?"

Holly shrugged. "It's not the romance of the century, but I like him. He likes me more than I like him, but that's the way it is right now. Besides, I don't see all that much of him because he works with his dad in the summer. His parents own a little restaurant over in Tarpon Springs."

"You used to live for the day you'd have a boyfriend."

"It's not as important as I once thought."

Raina's cell phone played music foretelling that Kathleen was calling. She flipped it open. "Hey, Kathleen. What's up?"

"I need to talk. I just found out that my mom's going to marry this Stewart guy. Can you believe it?"

seventeen

"WHAT'S THE PROBLEM with your mom wanting to get married?" Raina asked. She and Holly had driven straight to Kathleen's when they had finished at the hospital for the day. Mary Ellen had gone out for the evening with Stewart.

Kathleen restlessly paced the living room floor. "Hel-*lo*—she hardly knows this man!"

"Actually, marriage sounds logical to me," Raina offered. "You're going off to college. She'll be alone. Why *not* get married?"

"I'm going to USF—right down the street. I'd planned to live at home to save money."

"So?" Holly asked.

Kathleen threw her arms up in disgust. "I don't want to live in the same house with this . . . this stranger!"

"He won't be a stranger. He'll be her husband," Holly said.

"Your stepfather," Raina added.

This brought Kathleen to a standstill. "I don't want a stepfather."

Raina and Holly exchanged glances. Kathleen stood facing them, tears of frustration brimming. Holly took one of her hands, Raina the other, and they sat her between them on the overstuffed sofa. "What exactly did your mother tell you?"

"Th-that she loved him. This man. This stranger."

Raina ventured, "She's been alone a long time. It's no fun being alone."

The poignancy of Raina's words wasn't lost on Holly, but she focused on Kathleen. "I thought you liked Stewart. You once told us that he made your mother happy."

"He's all right," Kathleen said grudgingly. "I—I just never thought about him moving in."

"You have somebody to love; why shouldn't she?" Holly asked.

"She's just always loved my dad."

"Who's been dead since you were eight," Holly said tenderly, remembering how Mary Ellen had talked to her about the loss of Kathleen's father. "Shouldn't she get a shot at being happy again?"

Kathleen sniffed. "They both have MS. How are they going to take care of each other?"

Raina said, "You know, girlfriend, that's not your problem. They've discussed it, I'm sure, and they've worked something out. It's their lives. Don't be a roadblock."

"If it were *your* mother—"

"I'd be speechless," Raina said wryly.

"Is this wedding anytime soon?" Holly asked.

"She hasn't said."

"Maybe they're just talking, not really planning."

"Does Stewart come with baggage?" Raina asked.

"What do you mean?"

"Baggage—children, ex-wives."

"He was married once, a long time ago, but when he got MS, she left him. No kids."

"Then you don't ever have to worry about anyone moving into *your* room, do you?"

Kathleen looked exasperated. "You make it sound so cut-and-dried. I just don't want my mother to make a mistake."

"She's not a kid, Kathleen," Raina said. "Maybe you should just feel happy for her and let her go her own way. You have Carson, don't you?"

"That's different."

"How so?"

Kathleen had no answer.

"Let her decide who and what she wants. It's only fair."

"What idiot thought up Valentine's Day?" Raina asked. "He should be shot." She and Holly had been poring over their books in a back section of the local library for hours.

"The guy died years ago," Holly said, looking up. "He's some saint now, I think."

"I hate him."

Ironically, Holly had received a sweetly sappy card from Chad that afternoon by regular mail, along with two e-cards. A momentous occasion, because it was the first honest and real Valentine she'd ever received from a guy. Raina had been flooded with Valentine's Day cards and gifts all her life, many from Hunter.

Raina doodled a heart on her notebook, scribbled a line down the middle to signify its breaking, then slashed lines through the entire drawing. "Emma sent me a card," she said.

"That's nice. How is she doing?"

"We e-mail a lot these days. She's still doing well with the transplant. She and Jon-Paul love each other so much. I know how it feels to love someone like that."

Holly didn't. She liked Chad, but she didn't feel in love with him. Not with all her heart. Looking across the study table at Raina, Holly saw that she was slipping into melancholy. She shut her book. "You know what? I'm getting a craving for some ice cream. What do you say we knock off and go have sundaes at Udder Delight?"

Raina blinked and gathered up her books. "Sounds like a good plan." When they got to the car, she turned to Holly. "Thanks."

"For what?"

"For keeping me from going into a tailspin."

Holly shrugged, grinned. "You may be less grateful if you get on the scale tomorrow."

"Doubtful. Tomorrow's the day *after* Valentine's Day. I can't wait."

On Valentine's Day evening, Stewart Milita invited Kathleen and Carson to join him and Mary Ellen at a fancy restaurant. Carson picked up Kathleen at her house. "You don't look real happy to be doing this," Carson said as they drove to the restaurant where Mary Ellen and Stewart were waiting.

"Does it show?"

"You're wearing a sign on your face."

"I'll try to take it off before we get there."

Carson shook his head. "What's so bad about eating a free meal?"

She crossed her arms. "I don't like the man all that much."

"Then why are we going?"

"Because Mom wants me to go. She's—well, all glowy. It's dumb."

"Don't I make you all glowy? You make *me* all glowy."

"Be serious. This is my mother here. She says she loves this guy and that they're talking about getting married."

"Sounds kind of normal to me."

"Who's going to take care of them?"

"They will take care of each other. Isn't that how it's supposed to work?"

Carson didn't get it either, and Kathleen didn't have the time or patience to explain it. They were at the restaurant all too soon. Once inside, Stewart stood and waved them over. He was a tall man with silvery hair, older than Kathleen's mother, but not by much. He shook Carson's hand. Kathleen watched, seeing the slight wobble of Stewart's body when he stood, the hand that trembled slightly when he gestured for them to sit. "We've got the two prettiest women in the room," Stewart told Carson.

Corny. Kathleen struggled not to do an eye roll. Her mother's smile was a hundred watts.

"True." Carson picked up his menu. "What's good?"

"We're having lobster for two," Mary Ellen offered with a giggle. "It's the Valentine's Day special. Get whatever you want."

I'm going to gag, Kathleen thought.

"Oh, look, babe, calamari," Carson said, pointing to the menu.

Kathleen felt her face redden. He was reminding her of their first date at the country club and how she'd innocently ordered the dish without knowing what it was. She'd been trying to impress Stephanie, who'd come by their table uninvited.

"I didn't know you liked squid," Mary Ellen said.

"Um—" Kathleen shot daggers at Carson.

"Don't care much for the stuff myself," Stewart said, "but if you like it, I'll get us an order." Before she could protest, he called over the waiter and put in the order.

Kathleen fumed, but she checked her attitude. Her mother and Stewart seemed oblivious to her mood anyway. Carson had the gall to wink at her over the calamari when it arrived. She chewed on a couple of pieces, but Carson ate most of it.

Conversation flowed easily among Stewart, her mother and Carson. When Stewart heard that Carson wanted to be an EMT, he told long-winded stories about a friend of his who was a tech in New Jersey.

Mary Ellen asked Carson about his parents.

Stewart asked Kathleen about school.

At some point the meal was finished, and the waiter whisked away the plates and reappeared with a small cream cake, four glasses and a bottle of champagne. "Just a sip for the kids," Stewart told the waiter, which annoyed Kathleen instantly. *The kids?* She wasn't *his* kid.

When the champagne had been poured and handed around, Stewart and Mary Ellen gave each other beaming looks. "Stewart has something he wants to say."

Wait for it, Kathleen thought, knowing the announcement was the real reason for the dinner invitation.

Stewart fumbled in his jacket pocket, pulled out a ring box and handed it to Mary Ellen. She opened it, extracted the ring and handed it to him, and he slipped it on her finger. "Will you marry me, Mary Ellen McKensie?"

Mary Ellen's eyes shimmered. "Of course I will."

Kathleen's heart raced like an out-of-control train.

Stewart turned to Kathleen. "Your mother and I wanted you to share this moment with us, Kathleen. I want you to know that I love her with all my heart. And I will take care of her for as long as we live."

Kathleen felt Carson's gaze on her, felt her mother's joy like an aura around the table. In her mind's eye, she saw her father fade away into the background. Tears filled her eyes. "Congratulations," she said tightly.

She allowed them to think her tears were because she was happy for them, but deep down, she felt a minor shift in the earth's movement. Things would never be the same in her home again. Her mother was moving on, and without fear of what tomorrow would bring. Kathleen felt numb. She couldn't hold back the future.

"Have you set a date?" Carson asked, shaking Stewart's hand.

Mary Ellen said, "Probably in September. After Kathleen gets settled in college. The wedding won't be large. We'll invite the members of our support group, your family, Vicki and the Harrisons, of course. I'll want Kathleen to stand up with me."

Kathleen forced a smile. "Sure, Mom."

Later in the car, before starting the engine, Carson put his arms around Kathleen and kissed her. "You did good, babe. Didn't throw a fit, or anything. You okay?"

"I'm getting used to the idea." She pulled back. "She'll be a Milita and me a McKensie. Think about it. She won't even have to change the monograms on her towels."

Holly was late and hurtling through the hospital halls at a run. She skidded to a stop at the door of the recreation room on pediatrics, only to find that all the kids had been returned to their rooms. She'd missed the afternoon art session. She heaved a sigh and leaned against a wall to catch her breath. Mrs. Graham stepped out of her office. "Holly, I've been looking for you. Could you come in here, please?"

Holly blew out air and hurried into the closet-sized office of her supervisor. "I'm so sorry, Mrs. Graham, but I couldn't find a parking space, and then only two elevators were working in the lobby—"

Mrs. Graham looked grim. "I don't care about that, Holly. I have something to tell you."

"What is it?"

"Susan from oncology came in today with some difficult news." Mrs. Graham picked up a paper from her desk. "It seems that Ben Keller has been readmitted. He's relapsed and is being treated for leukemia again."

eighteen

WITH A SICK feeling of dread, Holly hurried to the oncology wing, asked for Ben's room number at the nurses' station, steeled herself and entered his room.

Ben's face lit up as soon as he saw her. "Holly!"

He held open his arms and she gathered him up and hugged him. "How are you doing?" She tousled his hair, regrown thick and blond after he'd recovered from his last chemo treatments. He would probably lose it all again.

"I got sick. Doctor says I have to come back and get more medicine." Ben looked resigned to his fate.

Holly's heart went out to him. "I'm still working here, so I can be with you. If you want, that is."

"Will you still be my girlfriend?"

"You're my main man." She swallowed around a lump in her throat. "Is your mom with you?"

"She's getting some tea, then she's coming back."

Relieved that Ben wouldn't have to spend so much time by himself this visit, she said, "Well, I can stay with you too sometimes. Maybe we'll get ice cream again. Do you still like ice cream?"

"Sure." Ben offered a sweet smile.

Ben's mother came into the room. "Holly. You heard."

"The nurse told me."

Beth-Ann set down a paper sack and offered Ben some candy. "I'm going to talk to Holly in the hall, honey. I won't be long."

Ben picked up the TV remote. "Cartoons are on."

"I'll see you tomorrow," Holly told Ben, and went with Beth-Ann into the corridor. Ben's mother was young and shy. Now she looked haggard. "I—I'm really sorry," Holly said.

"I thought he was home free. Then a few weeks ago, I saw some bruising on his little legs. He told me he fell off his bike, but deep down, I knew. My mom moved in to watch Howie, and I brought Ben yesterday. A few tests confirmed the worst."

"When will he start chemo?"

"Tomorrow." Beth-Ann's soft Southern accent made the single word sound forlorn. "It's just that every time he goes out of remission, it's less likely the chemo will work."

"How about a bone marrow transplant?" Holly was thinking of Raina and Emma.

"We've all been tested—even little Howie—but none of us is a match. That's kind of crazy, but it's true. So he's been registered in the National Bone Marrow Donor Program. Maybe someone will match him."

Holly saw that Ben's options were narrowing. Knowing how far he and Beth-Ann lived from Parker-Sloan, she asked, "So, will you be able to stay with him the whole time?"

"So long as Mama can keep up with Howie. I'll probably run home a couple of times a week 'cause I don't want little Howie to forget me. Plus Mama's getting up there in years, and chasing a toddler around is hard work." Beth-Ann smiled. "Ben's daddy is driving extra shifts. We have insurance, but the bills mount up. We're almost out of major medical benefits."

Holly had never considered that their insurance would run out. "I'll stay with Ben whenever you need me to."

Beth-Ann smiled kindly. "You're a good person, Holly. One of the nurses told me what happened to your brother, and I'm real sorry."

Holly nodded, not trusting herself to speak. She said goodbye and returned to her shift on pediatrics, but just as soon as she could, she left for home. She made it inside the house before the dam broke and she started crying.

"Honey, what's wrong?" her mother asked, meeting her in the foyer. "Come sit on the sofa and tell me what's happened."

Holly told her mother about Ben, but as she did, her tears of sadness turned into tears of anger. When she stopped to blow her nose, she announced, "You were right all along, Mom. Everything you said about God is true. He's nothing but a big joke!"

Evelyn looked startled. "I—I never said that."

"Sure you did. In so many words. I mean, if he really cared about us, then why do little kids like Ben have to get sick?" She almost added, ". . . *and why did Hunter die?*" but checked herself at the last moment. "I'm like you now, Mom—I don't believe in God anymore. Going to church and thanking him for everything is for stupid people."

Evelyn said nothing. She just held Holly, rocked her, stroked her hair. Holly started to pull away, realizing that she was too old, too mature to be crying like a baby on her mother's shoulder. But her mother resisted, so Holly remained in her embrace, suddenly realizing that it was the first time Evelyn had held her since that night in Hunter's room. Holly shut her eyes and breathed in the familiar scent of her mother's skin, relishing the comfort she felt in her mother's arms.

*   *   *

"Good news, girlfriend!" Raina dropped her books with a thud on the library study table across from Holly, who was already doing homework. "I've pulled all my grades out of the toilet. Mr. Crowder's giving me a D, but all my other teachers have told me I've come up to Cs and C-pluses."

The library was decorated for St. Patrick's Day, with green four-leaf clover and leprechaun cutouts strung everywhere. Over the central desk a rainbow hung, dipping into a pot of gold on one end. A sign read FIND YOUR GOLD IN BOOKS.

Holly grinned. "Way to go. And don't sweat it—Crowder gives everybody Ds."

"Not you."

Holly shrugged self-consciously. "I give him my evil eye all the time. Turns him into a robot to do my will."

Raina looked thoughtful. "We're getting close to the end, aren't we?"

It took Holly a second to grasp her meaning. "You mean graduation?"

"Exactly. Have you picked a college?"

"I've gotten a few acceptance letters from state universities, but nothing's ringing my chime."

"You still irked about Kathleen going to USF? And me—well, I'm not sure what I'll be doing."

"That tantrum I pitched was so lame," Holly

confessed, remembering. How could she ever have gotten into such a snit with friends as good as hers? "You can always start at the community college and transfer in a year or two."

"I'd have to go in on academic probation." Raina shook her head. "I'm still thinking about a plan. At least Mom's backed off my case since she sees me working harder for my grades."

"That's good. Who needs to be infected with Mom hassle?"

Raina giggled. She opened her book, read a few paragraphs, then looked over at Holly. "How's Ben doing?"

Holly sighed and slumped in her chair. "Sick as a dog. But I stop by to see him whenever I'm at the hospital. I read to him, give his mom a break. The grandmother brought Howie by the other day. He's so cute. And he cried when it was time to leave Ben and his mom."

"How long will Ben be there this time?"

"Until they get him into remission. It could take a long time."

"Poor guy."

"Beth-Ann told me that their whole church was praying for Ben and that she thought God was going to heal him." Holly scoffed. "As *if.*"

Raina arched an eyebrow. "You don't believe it?"

"I don't believe *any* of that stuff anymore."

"Doesn't that upset your parents?"

"Oh, Dad still preaches the party line, but I think Mom's over the hump of illusion."

"I'm surprised."

"Why? You've never believed it. Hasn't affected your life."

Raina toyed with the pages of her book, looking troubled. "But I always respected that you believed it."

They were silent, and the sounds of shuffling feet, books plopping onto tables and the squeaky-wheeled library cart filled the time. Finally, Raina said, "Hunter wouldn't like knowing that you stopped believing, you know. He wouldn't like it at all."

Kathleen said, "Prom's coming in a few weeks. You and Chad want to double with me and Carson?"

Holly was caught off guard. She'd not given her senior prom a single thought. They were eating lunch in the commons area of the high school, rather than in the cafeteria, because it was Senior Privileges Day. "Good question. I don't know."

"Don't you want to go? You used to talk about it all the time."

"I used to talk about a lot of stuff that doesn't mean much to me now."

"But you have a boyfriend. And it *is* the prom."

"Are you going to Carson's prom too?"

"He said it didn't matter to him which one we went to, and told me to pick whichever one I wanted to attend, because he wasn't getting into a tux two times in one month."

Holly smiled. "And you picked ours. How loyal."

"I don't like the snobby crowd at Bryce."

"I guess you'll be getting a new dress."

"Absolutely. Mom's in a great mood these days, what with her engagement and all." Kathleen rolled her eyes. "I'm buying the coolest dress I can find. We could shop together," she added hopefully. "Do you want to go with Chad?" Kathleen asked suddenly, having doubts for the first time. "I mean, is there anyone else in the picture?"

"Ben, but I'd have to check him out of the hospital for the night and he'd have to stay up past his bedtime."

Kathleen took a bite of her sandwich. "Have you, um, kissed him yet? Chad, I mean."

"Nope. I don't think either one of us has gotten up the nerve. He's self-conscious about his CF. And I'm not sure I want to go there with him."

Kathleen recalled how much angst she'd suffered before kissing Carson. "Well, the first kiss is the hardest. After that, it's really fun."

"We'd go together, right?"

"Four peas in a pod."

"I guess Raina won't be going."

"Can't imagine it. Funny, you know—I always thought I'd be the one sitting home on prom night."

"Me too," Holly said.

Chad seemed overjoyed when Holly invited him to her prom, asking her more questions than she'd have thought possible, but she was patient with him, reminding herself that Chad was homeschooled and didn't know a lot about regular high school life. "Call Carson for more details," she said finally. "He knows all that guy stuff."

"I know enough to ask what color dress you're wearing."

"I'll let you know when I buy it."

He was quiet. "Thanks, Holly. It means a lot for you to ask me."

"We'll have fun," she said lightly, hoping he wouldn't read more into the invitation than she meant. No use in either of them getting psyched up for more than they might ever be able to give each other.

nineteen

EASTER CAME EARLY, and spring break was sched-
uled for the last week in March. The prom was
set for the second weekend in April. While most
of Holly's classmates drifted farther south to
beaches and parties, she intended to spend every
free minute at the hospital, along with Raina and
Kathleen, who had declined Carson's invitation
to head to Miami with him and some of his
friends.

"But what if that horrible Stephanie goes
and you're not there to protect your turf?" Raina
asked Kathleen when she told them.

"I guess I'll just have to trust him," Kathleen
said. "And besides, the party scene just isn't me.
We'd probably just fight the whole time."

"And—?" Holly asked, sensing there was
more to the story.

"And my mom won't let me go."

"Aha!" Raina said.

"I'm living at home; Mom still calls the
shots."

"Maybe we can go to one of the big new movies," Holly suggested. "Some good ones are opening Easter weekend."

"Suits me," Raina said. "Nothing else to do."

So they agreed to spend the holiday attending one movie after the other.

Holly was relieved because she had been dreading the Easter holidays. Easter Sunday had always been celebrated with new clothes, a sunrise church service and breakfast in the church fellowship hall served by the youth group, followed by the regular church service and then a huge meal at home with her family and many invited friends. Her mother cooked for days, preparing for the big feast. This year, everything was going to be different. Holly was too old for chocolate bunnies and baskets of colored eggs. What she wanted was for things to be the same as before Hunter's death. What she wanted was to not repeat the disastrous Christmas holiday.

When she drove home after her day-long shift on Thursday, she was surprised to open the front door to the aroma of cooking food. She found her mother in the kitchen busily preparing supper and putting away sacks full of groceries. "Good. You're home," Evelyn said. "Dinner's just about ready."

"You're cooking?"

"Don't looked so shocked. I still remember how." Evelyn lifted the lid on a frying pan and stirred the contents. "Help put things away. We're having Kevin and his wife and a few others over on Sunday. I got a huge ham, so you'll have to move things around to get it in the fridge."

Kevin was the youth director at their church and had been a good friend of Hunter's. Holly started unloading the bags. "You've got a lot of food here."

"It's going to be a big meal. Don't make plans on Saturday. I'll need your help."

"Um—what's happened?"

"What do you mean?"

"You—you just seem . . . different."

Evelyn slid a wooden spoon onto the stovetop. Her expression looked solemn but serene. "I've been doing a lot of thinking lately. And I think it's time I returned to the land of the living."

This was the mother Holly had been missing. "What . . . brought you back?"

Evelyn held Holly's gaze. "A moth. And you."

Holly almost said something flip, but the look on her mother's face was serious. She couldn't imagine how either she or a moth was relevant to her mother's change of heart, and couldn't quite decide on the explanation she wanted to hear first. After a second, she said, "Okay, I'm curious—how did a moth change you?"

Evelyn turned down the flame under the

frying pan, went to the kitchen table and pulled out a chair. "Sit."

Holly settled across from her mother and waited patiently while Evelyn gathered her thoughts.

"I was standing at my bedroom window the other day. I was alone and the house was quiet. Like a tomb. And then I heard this tapping sound and I looked down. I saw a moth frantically flapping its wings against the glass pane, trying to get outside. And I thought, 'Stupid bug. You can't go through solid glass.' I told the moth that it was useless; it would never get out that way." She half smiled. "Stupid me, huh? Talking to a moth. The moth was destroying itself, Holly. The fine powder of its wings was coming off on the glass, collecting on the windowsill, and without the powder, it wouldn't be able to fly, even if it got outside, which it wouldn't." Evelyn paused. "Then I realized that I was like that moth."

The image burned vividly in Holly's mind— the flailing moth, the sunlight pouring through the glass, beckoning to the bug's primitive instinct to soar toward the bright light.

Moisture filled Evelyn's eyes. "All these months, I've been beating my wings against the glass, trying to find a way out of all this pain, and blaming God for taking away my son. I can't bring Hunter back. Hating God won't do it. Isolating myself from my family won't do it. He's gone from this life forever."

She took a deep shuddering breath. Holly's eyes filled with tears of empathy. What her mother had said was true. Hunter would never return to them. "But," Evelyn added firmly, "although I won't see him here, on this side of time, I still believe that I will see him on the other side. In heaven."

The room went quiet until only the bubbling of the pan on the stove could be heard. Outside, a car horn blared. Across the room, the refrigerator hummed. For her mother, nothing had changed and everything had changed. Holly longed to feel the same kind of revelation, but she was confused. Was heaven even real? Could she believe in such a place again? It seemed so childlike, so much like a fairy tale.

Evelyn said, "Ironic, isn't it—how the most ordinary things in life can shine a spotlight into the darkest places of a person's heart and bring understanding."

"And what about me, Mom? What did I do to change things for you?"

Evelyn plucked a napkin from the holder on the table and blew her nose. "After we talked that day you told me about Ben, I realized that I had given you a wrong impression."

"What was that?"

"I haven't lost my *faith* in God, Holly. But I did lose my *way* to him. In spite of how I've acted, I still believe in him. I'm mad at him—furious—but I still believe. God is my only hope for going on with this life, in order to enjoy the next one. I—I don't want you to lose your faith because of me."

"I'm not so sure I feel the same way as you do, Mom." It was a difficult thing for Holly to admit, but she wanted to be honest too. She expected a lecture, and braced for it.

Instead, Evelyn said, "I can't give you faith, Holly. I can raise you in faith. I can teach you what I believe, but faith is for you alone to discover."

"I'm not sure what I believe anymore."

"That's fine. You will eventually." Evelyn reached across the table, clasped Holly's hand. "I love you, Holly. With all my heart. I'm so sorry I checked out on you and your father for so long."

Holly shrugged self-consciously. "I knew you were hurting. It's okay."

"We all were hurting."

Holly searched the raw exposed emotion etched into her mother's features. She saw tiny lines at the corners of her mother's eyes and mouth. She saw gray hairs nestled in the mass of dark hair around her face. When had that happened? Holly cleared her throat. "What happened to the moth?"

"I caught it in a plastic cup, opened the screen and tossed it at the sky. It seemed the right thing to do."

For days, Holly thought about their conversation, long after Easter was gone and April had come. She was glad that her mother had found a way out of her self-imposed exile and pain. But for Holly, it was more complex. The loss of Hunter had shaken her world in more ways than just the horrible loss of her brother. She no longer felt safe with the things she had believed in while growing up. She no longer felt protected and comfortable with her parents' values, or their beliefs. The fact that she attended church with God-fearing parents did not shelter her from evil. That childhood world was gone now. In its place was uncertainty, a sense of indecision, of being stalled, of wanting to know what to think and believe, but of being unable to figure out where all the pieces fit that shaped the new and unexplored configuration of her life.

twenty

"You look beautiful."

The expression on Chad's face as he said the words made Holly blush. Dressed in her floor-length prom dress of midnight blue, she *felt* beautiful. She took the corsage he held out, a cluster of pale pink baby roses, and handed it to her mother so she could pin it onto the tiny strap of the dress.

"Stand here," her father said. "Let me get another picture."

"Daddy! We've already taken a ton of pictures. Carson and Kathleen are waiting."

"One more won't hurt." Mike focused the lens and fired off two shots. "Be careful," he added as Chad reached for the door. "And call us when you get to that party."

"We will," Holly sang over her shoulder. Once the prom was over at midnight, a "safe" party was being sponsored out at the lake house of a senior's parents. A hot local band had been hired, and chaperones would be highly visible to make sure that no one drank anything stronger than soda. Breakfast would be served too. Plenty of kids were skipping the party, but it was the only way that Holly would be allowed to stay out all night, so she and her friends were going.

Outside, Chad took her hand. At the end of her driveway, a white limo purred, courtesy of Carson. The driver opened the door and Holly and Chad climbed inside. "Wow," Carson said. "You look great, Holly."

The couples were sitting across from each other on plush white leather seats in the air-conditioned car. Soft music played. Kathleen said, "Fabulous, girlfriend."

"Right back at you," Holly said. Kathleen was dressed in a long pale aqua satin sheath, her red hair piled atop her head and sprinkled with glitter, and she wore pearl drop earrings. She looked sleek and sophisticated.

They had bought their dresses together during a marathon day of shopping, with Holly shuttling them to small, trendy boutiques instead of the big department stores.

"Cool wheels," Chad said.

"It's ours until the sun rises," Carson said. "Let's make the most of it." He dimmed the interior lights, opened an ice chest and extracted a bottle of sparkling cider. "I would have brought the real bubbly, but Dad went over the car with a microscope and then threatened the driver with a lawsuit if any booze appeared."

Kathleen patted his leg. "We'll survive, party boy."

He found glasses in a console and poured them each some of the sweet carbonated drink. They raised their glasses in a toast. "Here's to the most famous night of senior passage—the prom."

Holly locked gazes with Kathleen, and each knew what the other was thinking—if only Raina and Hunter were with them, the evening would be absolutely perfect. Hunter should have been there. *If only* . . .

Raina had signed on for an all-nighter at the hospital, going in at seven with the graveyard shift. A macabre way to spend prom night, she thought, but it was the way she'd wanted to spend it. The hospital was like a different place at night, amazingly busy, with staffers getting patients medicated and settled and making sure that all nonessential visitors were gone. By ten o'clock, the rooms were dark, hall lights had been dimmed, and nurses' stations glowed like small islands in a sea of semi-darkness. Vicki had told Raina that if she got sleepy, she should go to her office and nap on the sofa. She'd left a soft throw and a pillow, but Raina knew she wouldn't be using them.

She thought about Kathleen and Holly, pictured them having fun, and was glad for them. Two different boys had asked her, but she'd simply shaken her head. She'd not gone to Hunter's prom either because he'd taken early admission and had been away at college when his prom night rolled around. "We'll go to yours next year," he'd promised. Except, of course, they couldn't. No matter. She thought the event highly overrated anyway. And without Hunter—well, it mattered even less to her.

The prom was being held at the Don CeSar, one of St. Petersburg's oldest and most prestigious hotels, overlooking the bay. The main ballroom had been transformed into an undersea fantasy world with giant clamshells that opened and blew streams of bubbles high into the air. Tables draped in blue linen and lit with votives lined the room and clustered in a circular arrangement at one end. A dance floor filled the other end. A live band and DJ worked in the stage area. "Who picked these guys?" Carson asked, frowning.

"The prom committee, but they were closely supervised, and anybody with a nose ring was automatically disqualified," Kathleen said with a shrug.

Carson looked disgusted. "They're not very good."

"Ambiance," Kathleen joked, kissing his cheek.

A giant movie-style screen provided a

backdrop on one wall. Underwater scenes floated past, showing bright schools of fish and forests of coral. "So when does Nemo arrive?" Holly asked.

"Good one," Carson said, giving her a high five.

"Will you two make an attitude adjustment?" Kathleen said.

Chad hooked his arm around Holly's waist. "Let's dance."

She was nervous about dancing with him, but they went onto the floor and he took her in his arms because the band was playing a slow song. He nuzzled her ear, sending shivers up her back. "I think everything looks cool."

"You're just being nice."

"Nothing could bother me tonight. We're together."

She wasn't sure how to respond, so she skirted the topic. "How's your sailboat?"

"In dry dock for a coat of paint. Me and my dad are doing it because she's small and we can work on her together." He pulled back. "Would you like to sail with me again when she's back in the water? You're good at the tiller."

"We'll see. Maybe," she added when he looked disappointed.

"What about next year? Will you stay in Florida?" He sounded hopeful.

"I'm not sure yet. Acceptance letters are arriving, but I haven't decided where I want to go to college. How about you? You going to college?"

"Probably USF, St. Pete campus. I might get an apartment because the commute's too far for everyday driving. I can manage my CF without my mommy, you know."

She felt her cheeks redden. He wasn't an invalid, and she might have given him the impression that she thought so.

"If we both stay in state come this fall, maybe we can see each other. On occasion," he added quickly. "I know you don't want to be tied down."

"I don't know what I want," she said truthfully as the song ended. "I'm still looking for what it is. When I find out, I'll let you know."

By midnight, the hospital was very quiet for the most part, and Raina was drifting from floor to floor trying to figure out where to spend the rest of the night. The emergency room was full, but she didn't like hanging there. Nor did she like the ICU floors. Too much life and death going on. She ended up on the floor with the labor rooms and was walking the hall toward the newborns' nursery when a woman called to her from a doorway. "Hey, you, Pink Angel."

Raina turned and saw a woman wearing scrubs. "Yes?"

"Raina?" The woman didn't wait for confirmation. "I remember you from when you helped in the nursery. I'm Cathy, a midwife. Listen, this place is hopping tonight and we're short-staffed. Must be a full moon. Every room is full, and this gal is about to deliver. Can you help?"

Raina entered the labor room, where a young woman was experiencing advanced labor. Usually, a husband or boyfriend was with the mother-to-be, but this woman had only the midwife.

Cathy said, "She's had an epidural. The baby's coming fast and we won't make it to the delivery room."

An epidural meant that the lower half of the patient's body had been anesthetized. "What can I do?" Raina asked.

"Glove up. As soon as this little guy's born, I'll hand him off to you. Take him over to that isolette"—she pointed to a clear plastic bassinet on the other side of the room—"and make sure he stays warm. As soon as I take care of the mother, I'll come clean him up."

Raina had never seen a baby being born, and couldn't see much now because the midwife told her to stand behind her, but she heard the young mother moaning and heard Cathy say, "I see his head! Push, Sandra. Push hard."

Seconds later, Raina heard a baby's wail.

"A beautiful boy," Cathy said. She clamped off the umbilical cord, turned and handed the squalling, bloodied baby to Raina.

Raina rushed the infant to the isolette,

placed him gently on the pile of clean cloth and turned on the warming light attached to the side. He kept crying and kicking, as if angry about being ejected from his cocoon of dark warmth into the cold, too-bright world. She wrapped him in a blanket, as she'd been taught, and he quieted. His wide-open eyes were the familiar slate gray of all newborns' eyes, and as he stared up at her, she thought of the infant who had died in her arms. Unlike that baby, this little guy looked whole and perfect. "Welcome to life," she whispered, feeling an elation she had not experienced for a long, long time.

Holly and Chad walked barefoot and hand in hand along the beach behind the hotel. Light spilled from the windows and music floated from the sprawling tiled patio where couples danced and lounged. A full moon left a path of light on the calm water and small waves flowed in, tugged at the sand, flowed back. "I always plan to live near the ocean," Chad said. "How about you?"

"I've never lived anyplace except Tampa, but I'm pretty sure I won't be anyplace where it snows."

"You don't like snow?"

"Not especially. Give me the beach anytime."

"When I die, I want to be buried at sea," he said absently.

She had no response, realizing that he'd

given the idea some thought. How many kids their age had? She faced the salt water, studied the wide, brilliant path of light the moonlight made. "Wouldn't it be wonderful if we could walk on that strip of water and right up onto the moon?"

"Yes," Chad said. "It would be wonderful. If I could walk there with you."

She looked up at him, at the planes of his face swathed in the light. His eyes were dark pools. Curls of his black hair spilled onto his forehead. Her heartbeat quickened. "It's a long walk to the moon," she said, her voice barely a whisper.

"Not nearly long enough, if we're going there together."

He cupped her face between the palms of his hands. His skin felt warm and made her cheeks hot. He bent down, and hesitated for only a moment. Her heart had gone crazy, pounding so loudly in her ears that it drowned out the sound of the sea. She rose on bare tiptoes, closed her eyes and received his mouth as it closed softly over hers. The taste of him was sweet and filled her senses like the heady scent of the roses pinned to her dress. His lips lingered and she raised her arms, wrapped them around his neck, pressed him closer. Her last coherent thought was that Kathleen had been wrong—the first kiss wasn't the hardest. It was the most wonderful.

* * *

The long white limo drove Holly and her friends home after breakfast at the lake house. Holly didn't remember the ride; she was asleep, curled up on the seat in Chad's arms. She only remembered being gently shaken awake. "You're home," Chad whispered in her ear.

"Already?" She stretched lazily.

The driver opened the door, and Holly poked Kathleen and Carson, wound around each other like sleeping puppies on the other seat, and said goodbye. Outside, the air was humid and her eyes had to adjust to the sunny morning light. A car she didn't recognize was in her driveway. Chad walked her to the door, kissed her lightly and said, "I'll call later today." She went inside, still dreamy, half-asleep. In the foyer, she saw her parents, and with them, a man. He looked familiar, but why?

Her father said, "Holly, you remember Detective Gosso?"

Holly's mind snapped awake and she was fully alert. "I remember."

The detective looked somber but also satisfied. He said, "I came to tell your family that we've caught the man who killed your brother."

twenty-one

THE MAN'S NAME was Jerry Collins. He was twenty-two and had spent most of his life in and out of trouble with the law. His juvenile rap sheet was "as long as your arm," according to Gosso, but the law had never been able to keep him under lock and key—until now. According to the detective, Collins had fled the area after the killing and had only recently returned. He'd been arrested during a burglary, and a routine check of his prints revealed his record and also his presence at the restaurant.

"Our team has spent many hours putting together a case against this perp concerning your brother's killing. When I started laying it out for him, he confessed," Gosso told Holly's family. "Said he was coming off a high and looking for money for another fix. He never showed an ounce of remorse."

"What happens now?" Mike asked.

"He'll be arraigned. The DA's charging him with murder—a capital offense."

Evelyn glanced at Mike. "The death penalty?"

"It's on the table, but it will be up to a jury. He'll have a court-appointed attorney. Don't expect his trial to happen quickly," he added.

"Do you know when he'll be arraigned?"

"I'll call you as soon as I know."

Evelyn squared her jaw. "We'll go to the arraignment. I want to see this animal who murdered our son."

Holly looked at her mother's face, saw determination there, saw her father put his arm around her shoulders.

"Just let us know when," he said.

Gosso nodded. "I will."

Collins was arraigned on the first Wednesday in May, when Holly had less than two weeks of school remaining. She'd announced that she wanted to go to the courthouse also, even though it meant missing Senior Fun Day. Raina and Kathleen came too. "For moral support," Kathleen said.

"For justice," Raina said, her eyes full of hurt.

The government building was awash with people, all there on some kind of business or other. The courtroom, one of five, was crowded with spectators who changed continuously as their relatives' or friends' cases were called before the judge sitting high up at a dark wooden desk.

Behind him on the wall was the seal of the State of Florida; on either side were flags of the United States and Florida.

Detective Gosso showed up and sat with Holly and her family and friends on the spectators' benches near the front of the courtroom. "This may take a while," he explained. "The judge has a full docket."

"We'll wait," Evelyn said, her eyes bright with unshed tears.

Raina looked pale; Kathleen, subdued. Holly sat shoulder to shoulder with her parents, feeling as if they were a solid wall, braced for the ordeal ahead.

People charged with crimes passed before the judge in a monotonous stream, all with attorneys to speak for them. Holly thought the judge looked bored. And then the clerk announced a number and Gosso sat up straighter. Holly's heart heaved as a man was led into the room. Jerry Collins wore a bright orange jumpsuit and manacles on his wrists and ankles. His head had been shaved and only a dark stubble remained. His attorney, a young man in a rumpled suit, stood with him. On the other side of the room stood a tall woman in a business suit. "The prosecutor," Gosso whispered.

The clerk read the charges: burglary and murder in the second degree.

"How do you plead?" the judge asked.

"Not guilty," Collins's attorney said.

"Routine. Standard," Gosso told the Harrisons when they looked at him.

The prosecutor said, "The state recommends no bail, Your Honor. Mr. Collins is a flight risk."

"So ordered." The judge banged his gavel. "Next case."

Collins was led out. Holly felt cheated. She'd wanted him to beg for his life. At the door, Collins glanced out into the courtroom. Holly glared at him. He was thin, wasted-looking, but what struck her most was that his eyes looked dead. And then he was gone.

"That's it?" Raina asked.

"For now," Gosso said. He walked them out into the hall.

A reporter materialized, but Gosso waved her away. "Give these people some peace," he barked. "Come back when the perp goes to trial."

The reporter scowled, but backed away.

Mike shook the detective's hand. "We appreciate all you've done. I know you didn't have to come here today."

"I wanted to. I've been a detective for twelve years and I've put a lot of bad guys away. But in 2001, I lost my brother, a fireman, in the World Trade Center when the second tower fell. Until then I never knew what it was like to be a victim. You feel helpless and angry. You just want to take the bad guy down, but you can't." Gosso's gaze turned sorrowful. "I wanted to get this one for you. For your son."

"Thank you," Evelyn said.

Holly watched him walk away.

She blinked in the harsh light of the afternoon sun when they came out of the building. The whole arraignment seemed anticlimactic. Holly felt adrift, aimless. "Now what?" she asked.

"Let's go have pizza," Mike said.

"I don't—" Evelyn started.

"We all need to eat." He ushered the whole group to his SUV and drove to a pizza parlor, once a favorite haunt of Hunter's, in their part of town. The wonderful smells made Holly realize that she was hungry, and once they had settled in a booth and ordered, she began to feel less numb. Raina began to look more relaxed, as did Holly's parents, and Kathleen less scared.

When the pizzas came, they ate and talked, sharing stories about Hunter, memories of him as a child, a boyfriend, a brother, a friend. They laughed, they cried. And magically, the strain of the day lifted. The image of the courtroom, and of the villain who had changed their lives, began to fade. In its place were the warm, sweet memories of the boy they had all loved. And so tragically lost.

*   *   *

On Saturday, Kathleen was at work in the gift shop with Bree, setting out floral arrangements for delivery, when Carson hurried in looking for her. Kathleen beamed at him, but his face was serious. "What's wrong?"

"Um—we need to talk."

"Can it wait until I get off?"

"I'd rather talk right now." He glanced at Bree. "In private."

Bree shrugged, gave an affirming smile. "Go on. I can handle things here."

Kathleen felt growing concern as she walked with Carson into the hospital's huge atrium. He wouldn't have insisted unless something important was going on. He found a small table in the coffee bar and sat her down. He licked his lips. "I've just come up from the ER."

Her heart thudded with dread. "Go on."

"Steffie was in a car wreck. She hit a tree and went through the windshield."

"Oh no! How is she?"

"Alive, but cut up pretty badly."

Kathleen saw the concern in Carson's eyes. She wouldn't have wished a car wreck on anyone, not even Stephanie Marlow. "Did the ER call you?"

"Steffie asked them to call my mother, and Mom called me. Her parents aren't around. I guess there wasn't anyone else to call."

"That's so sad."

Carson shook his head in disgust. "She was almost hysterical. I calmed her down as best I could, but she's still pretty scared. She could have called her agent, but she doesn't want her to know about the accident yet. Not until the plastic surgeon stitches her up."

Kathleen realized how serious the accident was for the girl. Her face was her fortune. "How bad is it?"

"Her nose is broken and there are lots of cuts on her face, some pretty deep. Mom called one of her doctor friends—she says he's the best. I left when he came in." Carson brooded. "It was a stupid accident."

"Do you know how it happened?"

"The police said she was alone, coming home from an all-night party. She'd been drinking, took a corner too fast, skidded, hit a tree. Really stupid of her. To drink and drive," he said. "The cops are going to charge her."

Kathleen wondered if he had taken the leap to understanding that he had often done the same thing and that this might have happened to him too. "Was she wearing a seat belt?"

He shook his head. "Another dumb call."

"I hope she'll be all right."

Carson searched her face. "So you're not mad at me for going to see her?"

"No way. Why would you ask such a thing?"

He looked relieved, and she realized how troubled he was about coming to tell her. "I—um—just didn't want you to be upset."

She reached across the table, grabbed his hand. "You did the right thing. It's okay. She needs a friend." And as she said the words, she knew it was true. She wasn't jealous of Stephanie anymore. Whatever had happened between the girl and Carson was long gone and in the past.

He relaxed and flashed one of his sexy smiles. "I know girls who would have gloated."

"Pathetic."

They sat silently with the sounds of the hospital all around them. She thought about how much she liked him, and what a difference he'd made in her life.

He finally asked, "So, are you busy tonight?"

"Depends on who's asking."

He traced a line down the length of her arm with a finger, raising goose bumps on her skin. "Just me is asking."

"I'm yours," she said lightly, loading the words with a double meaning.

He winked. "I was the one who figured that out first, you know."

"*You* say," she answered coyly, without even a hint of self-consciousness.

With only days to go before the end of the school year and graduation, seniors didn't bother to attend classes past noon. Holly went to the hospital, not because she had to go for credit—she'd already earned that—but because she'd learned that Ben's treatment program had failed and that he'd been removed from all treatment except pain management. Medical science had failed, and Ben Keller, age eight, was dying.

twenty-two

BEN HAD BEEN moved into a more private area of the hospital, away from the hustle and bustle of his floor. His mother stayed with him round the clock. Relatives, neighbors, members of his family's church came to visit, and so did Holly. She wondered if Ben really knew what was happening to him. He slept a lot, ate little, seemed genuinely pleased and surprised to see the people who showed up. "No one's to say a sad word around him," Beth-Ann told all visitors sternly. "And no crying either. If you can't keep your feelings inside, then leave the room."

On one of Holly's visits, she found Beth-Ann standing in the hall and asked, "Is there really nothing more the doctors can do?"

"That's what they said."

"But even now, if he was taking chemo—"

"Wouldn't help any, and his daddy and I are real tired of seeing Benny suffer, of his being in pain all the time. That's not right. Us hanging on to him will only cause him more pain. He should be able to go in peace."

Tears welled in Holly's eyes, and Beth-Ann reached out for her. "It's his time, Holly. The Bible says there's a season for everything, and the season of Ben's life is ending. He's going home to be with Jesus. We have to let him go."

Holly understood all that. She knew that the faith of the Kellers was sustaining them, helping them come to terms with losing their child. She was glad for them, but for the life of her, she couldn't understand why Jesus needed a little boy in heaven. Or, for that matter, a big boy like Hunter. Heaven should be full of old people after they'd lived full lives on earth. Maybe some last-minute miracle would happen and spare Ben's life. *That* would make her feel good about God again!

"It's all right," Beth-Ann assured Holly in her soft Southern voice. "God knows best."

Holly didn't say what she really wanted to say about God being arbitrary. She just nodded and left the area.

The next evening, Holly ate a late supper in the cafeteria with Raina and Kathleen. They were trying to take her mind off what was happening to Ben. "Can you believe we're graduating *tomorrow*?" Kathleen asked.

The ceremony was to be held Saturday morning at the civic center.

"Not soon enough for me," Raina said. "I just made it out by the skin of my teeth, thanks to Holly."

"What?" Holly, distracted and toying with the food on her plate, looked up. "Did you ask me something?"

"I was giving you rave reviews on getting me to my diploma. Want me to say it again?"

Holly shook her head. "You worked hard. You deserve to walk."

"What are you doing after the pool party?" Kathleen asked.

Raina's mother was throwing a little get-together at the town house complex for some of the grads, their parents and a few close friends. "Celebration dinner with Mom at the Columbia," Raina said. "Want to come? Might keep the air from snapping between us."

"I thought things had smoothed out between you two."

"So much is different now." Raina shrugged, unable to put her feelings into words. "Can you come to dinner? Bring your mom and Stewart. Carson too."

"Thanks, but we can't. I promised Carson I'd go to his ceremony tonight. Then there's some big party at his house that his parents are throwing that we have to attend. At least Stephanie won't be invited. Carson said she decided not to finish at Bryce. Her grades were in the toilet anyway. She went back to South America to recover from her accident. He said her parents are finally getting a divorce, and he doesn't know if she'll ever come back to the States."

"We won't miss her, girlfriend, will we?" Raina said.

The noise of the cafeteria surrounded them as there was a lull in their conversation. Kathleen ended the break. "Oh, before I forget, Sierra asked me if we'd be volunteering this summer. She said she'd love for us to work on the carnival with her. Any thoughts?"

Holly remembered then that they'd all planned to help throw an anniversary carnival for the hospital and the patients. The summer before, Hunter had dressed as a clown and entertained everyone, passing out trinkets. "I don't know," she said listlessly.

"Me either. I've been thinking about making some changes in my life," Raina said mysteriously.

"I can," Kathleen said. "I'm working full-time in the gift shop, but I'll be glad to participate. Think about it. We once said we would."

Holly pushed her tray aside. "I'm going up to Ben's room. The nurses told me earlier that he had a bad day."

Raina caught her arm as she rose. "Are you

sure this death watch is something you really need to do?"

"Yes, I'm sure." Holly felt agitated, short-tempered.

Raina stood too. "Then we're coming with you."

"You don't have to."

"We're coming," Kathleen said.

Beth-Ann looked relieved to see Holly. "Ben's been asking for you. And his daddy and I need a quick break."

"I'll wait by his bed."

Holly and her friends slipped into the dim room. Outside the window, the lights of the city sparkled in the inky night. "Hey, buddy," Holly said, leaning over Ben.

His breathing sounded shallow and his skin looked colorless. His eyes slowly opened. "Holly?"

"Me and Raina and Kathleen."

He said something, but his voice was so soft, she asked him to repeat it.

His lips moved. "I'm scared, Holly."

Her heart twisted. "It's okay to be scared."

"No . . . I'm a big boy. I shouldn't be scared."

She knew that Beth-Ann had prepared him with talk of heaven and happiness and no more pain, but he was upset and she longed to comfort him. "What are you afraid of?"

"I'm scared of the dark."

She glanced around the room. The lights were turned down low. Raina shrugged. Kathleen reached over and turned up the light box on the wall behind the bed. "Is that better?"

He shook his head. "It's going to be dark inside that box they'll put me in. It's going to be dark under the ground, and I'm scared."

"I—it's not that way," she said slowly, her mind searching for a way to help him understand.

"I don't want everybody to go off and leave me alone in the dark." His voice sounded pitiful and very frightened. Tears pooled in the corners of his eyes.

Holly felt helpless. She had no way to make him understand that he'd have no awareness of the dark box or of being in the ground. She had no words to explain it. Nothing. And even if she did find the words, he wasn't capable of understanding. He was only a child and the complicated mechanics of death, of ceasing to exist in time and space, could not be explained to him. *Just as God had no way to explain to her why her brother had been murdered.* Like a searing light, the insight struck Holly with such force that she staggered.

"You all right?" Raina whispered, alarmed.

But Holly barely heard her. The realization about God reverberated in her head like an echo in an empty room. It wasn't that there was no explanation as to *why* kids died too young, or *why* people were murdered; it was that her mind was too limited, too simple to understand any explanation God could give her. God had not deserted her. He had been there all the time. She'd just been unable to see him through the fog of her pain and anger.

She focused again on Ben. He didn't need explanations, or platitudes. He needed tangible help. He needed something to calm his fears. "You know, Ben, I have an idea," she said. "All you need is a way to make the dark light." Suddenly recalling the donations that Hunter's boss had made to the carnival the summer before, she turned to Raina. "Do you still have the glow necklaces Hunter told me he gave you for safekeeping?"

Raina's eyes brightened. "Hunter gave me a ton of the things."

"Go get them."

As soon as Ben's parents returned to the room, Holly took them aside and told them what Ben had said and what she wanted to do for him. When Raina and Kathleen arrived, they carried a plastic box full of the flexible chemical lights. They all set to work snapping them around Ben's arms, his legs, his neck and even his head. Within fifteen minutes, he was aglow with bands of neon color—red, blue, hot pink, green and yellow. None of them had dry eyes as they worked, but Ben didn't seem to notice. He watched in fascination as the colors came to life on his body.

When they stepped aside, a nurse found a large mirror and held it up. He stared at himself, then sent them all a beautiful, peaceful smile. He was happy. Beth-Ann mouthed *Thank you* to Holly. She nodded, her heart bursting with a satisfied sense of accomplishment.

Holly saw Ben's eyelids growing heavy. She leaned over and said, "I'm leaving the rest of the container with your mama, so if one goes out, she'll put a new one on." She steadied her voice, then continued. "When you get to heaven, look for my brother, Hunter. When he sees you wearing all these necklaces, he'll come running to meet you. I know he will."

She and her friends left the room quickly, made it to a bathroom and there, holding on to one another, broke down crying. Yet as Holly wept, she realized that it didn't matter whether death came unexpectedly, as with Hunter, or with plenty of preparation time. The living, those left behind, were never truly ready for it. It came all the same, making holes in people's hearts and minds, pointing the way to eternity, where it could come for them no more.

* * *

"Don't forget, graduation's in a few hours," Raina said before she and Kathleen headed for home.

"I'll go home soon," Holly told them.

She looked in on Ben one more time in the early hours of the morning and was told that he'd slipped into a coma from which he would not awaken. On the bed, he lay wrapped in a hundred colorful lights, looking bright as a rainbow and bound for glory.

twenty-three

"I'll bet we're the only graduates to be doing *this* right after receiving our diplomas," Kathleen said ruefully.

She, Holly and Raina walked across the green lawn of the memorial garden in their lovely spring dresses, mortarboards and corsages in hand, toward the bronze plaque bearing Hunter's name. They hadn't discussed going; it had simply happened. After the ceremony and picture taking with their families, they'd looked at one another and in one telepathic thought knew what they were going to do. What they *had* to do.

"We'll be back in an hour or so," Raina had told her mother.

"But I've reserved the lounge at the pool house," Vicki had said. "Everyone's coming. You girls can't be late to your own party."

Holly had backed Raina up. "Go on, Mom and Dad. We'll be along soon. There's someplace we need to go first."

Her father had locked gazes with her and Holly had known instantly that he understood.

Raina had driven. The day was hot, brilliantly sunny, the eternal green of the grass shaded by live oaks dripping with Spanish moss. Birds chirped; the fountain in the center of the lake hissed water onto the calm surface, spreading falling rainbows as droplets caught the sunlight.

Holly found Hunter's grave and knelt in front of his plaque. Raina and Kathleen knelt on either side. "We made it, big brother," Holly said. "Bet you didn't think we would. I painted my nails bright orange too, and Dad never said a word." She fluttered her hands toward the ground, as if to show them off. "I'll bet you've met Ben by now. Isn't he a cutie? Take care of him."

She and her friends were driving to Crystal River Monday morning for Ben's funeral. Going would be sad, but she knew she'd make it through with her friends standing beside her.

Raina gazed down at the ground. "I miss you so much, Hunter. I still love you."

"But we didn't come here to be sad," Kathleen quickly inserted. "We came to say hello and leave you these." She placed her corsage on the metal plate. Holly and Raina did the same.

Holly sat back on her heels. "Dad gave me what's left of your college fund this morning. I've been accepted at the University of Miami—not too far away, but far enough." Her friends looked at her. Holly shrugged. "I made up my mind this morning, but I wanted to tell Hunter first."

Raina smoothed her dress and kept her gaze on the ground. "I have an announcement too. I'm going to live with Emma and Jon-Paul in Virginia."

"When did you decide this?" Kathleen looked shocked.

Holly just stared at Raina.

"Emma invited me a while back," Raina confessed. "I've thought about it for a long time, and I've decided to go. It's sad for me here. Everyplace I go reminds me of him." She ran her fingers over the raised letters of Hunter's name stamped on the brass.

"And your mother?" Holly asked.

"She's not crazy about the idea, but I'm eighteen and I want to know my sister better. She says she understands. But I don't care if she doesn't. It's something I have to do."

"Well, *blah!*" Kathleen blurted out; then she grumbled, "Boring Kathleen is staying put, Hunter. Going to good old USF. Being a bridesmaid." She looked at her friends. "You *are* planning to come to this wedding, aren't you? You aren't going to leave me alone to fend for myself, are you?"

Holly grinned. "You have Carson."

"Oh, like he's a big help. Who's going to do my hair? Counsel me on my attitude?"

"We'll phone it in if we have to," Raina said, patting Kathleen's hand.

Holly stood and so did the others. They lingered, staring down at Hunter's resting place, at the crisply clipped fringe of grass around the metal plaque, at their corsages already beginning to wilt in the humid heat. Sunlight shifting through the trees cast flickering shadows on the grass. Holly breathed in the warm, soft air, felt the cold knot in her chest begin to melt. Chad was coming to the pool party. He was probably already there, waiting for her. "We should go."

"Probably so," Raina said.

"Carson hates to wait around," Kathleen said. "The guy has no patience."

They glanced at each other. Holly said, "Ready?"

"Ready," Raina and Kathleen said in unison.

Together they stepped out onto an open patch of grass, hurled their mortarboards upward and watched as they turned, spun and tumbled together against the clear blue sky.

epilogue

THAT NIGHT, HOLLY couldn't sleep. The house was quiet, the parties over, the celebrations completed. She'd had a good time. She was a high school graduate, ready for the next phase of her life. And yet . . . *and yet* . . . She missed her brother. Hunter should have been there. He would have teased her, hugged her, ruffled her hair and, yes, prayed for her too.

Holly got up, turned on her desk lamp, reached into her drawer and pulled out her old diary. She hadn't written in it in ages, not since the previous summer. The blank pages stared up at her like black holes she couldn't fill because there was too much to write, or to remember. Still, she could start fresh. She considered where to begin—with the last days of school? The graduation ceremony? The party? *No*, she decided, as her heart spoke to her. She found a pen and began to write.

Dear Hunter,

All right, so I know you'll never read this, but I'm writing it anyway because it's not really for your sake, it's for mine. I never got to say goodbye. I just had to accept the fact that you were gone and never coming back. That's been hard. Even now, months later, I still expect to bang on the bathroom door and tell you to vacate because it's my turn. I expect to see you at the dinner table. I expect to grab the remote from you, make popcorn for us, cry on your shoulder when Dad and I disagree (which is happening less these days . . . aren't you proud of me?).

I never got to tell you a lot of things I meant to tell you but now can't. Maybe writing to you this way will help me face the rest of my life without my brother.

You were (I hate that I must write in the past tense) a pretty good brother . . . okay, a very good brother. I know I never told you that when I could, so I'm saying it now. You were always there for me, and I miss you a lot. I want to ask you for your take on things—like Chad, for instance. He says he loves me, Hunter. I like him. I really do. But love? I'm not ready for that. I tell him so, but it's like he doesn't hear me.

You loved Raina. And even though you and she were worlds apart on some things, you knew you loved her. I want to ask you, How did you know? Mom tries to give me advice, but it sounds corny. "Don't worry, you'll know." What kind of an answer is that? (Sorry, didn't mean to get sidetracked.)

There's just so much I want to talk to you about and tell you. Raina has had so much to deal with and has had a really hard time facing the world without you. There were days when I didn't think she would pull out of the black cloud that covered her. Yet she has. Sort of. You're a hard act to follow, H. I think it's going to be a long, long time before she falls in love again.

Mom had a rough time too. For a while I thought she would break apart. She was really mad at God. So was I. We're mostly over the being mad part, but Pastor Eckloes says that it might come up again, especially when the man who murdered you goes on trial. I know we're supposed to forgive him, but how? I'm not there yet.

Dad's managed best, but sometimes I see him with a faraway look on his face and I know he's thinking about you. Sometimes I see tears in his eyes. Then I have to look

*away because I can't stand seeing Dad cry.
Everyone misses you. Sometimes your old
friends stop by the house just to visit. I didn't
like it at first, but now it's easier to talk
about you and hear their stories about you.
(Did you really do a home video in Jeff
Johnson's garage in the eighth grade of an air
boy band?) And Kevin brought over a video
of a Bible talk you gave at camp one
summer. That one almost unraveled Mom
and Dad, but not me. I needed to hear you
say those things about love and faith.*

*Well, Hunter, it's getting late and I'm
finally winding down and getting sleepy. I
promised Kathleen and Raina we'd have a
day at Raina's pool tomorrow, just like old
times. Raina's moving in six weeks to live
with Emma, a good thing, I think, now that
I'm used to the idea. She would have moved
sooner but we've promised Sierra that we'd
be Pink Angels again this summer and help
her with the carnival set for July Fourth
weekend. It's going to take a ton of hard
work, but it was my idea, and my two best
friends are willing to help me. (What are
friends for?)*

*In truth, this won't be the last letter I
write to you. I know this because just doing
it has made me feel a whole lot better tonight*

already. So until next time, this is your favorite only sister signing off, still missing you, but feeling like you're a whole lot closer than the mansions of heaven. Please ask the angels to watch over us.

Holly

About the Author

Lurlene McDaniel began writing inspirational novels about teenagers facing life-altering situations when her son was diagnosed with juvenile diabetes. "I want kids to know that while people don't get to choose what life gives to them, they do get to choose how they respond."

Her many novels, which have received acclaim from readers, teachers, parents and reviewers, are hard-hitting and realistic but also leave readers with inspiration and hope.

Lurlene McDaniel lives in Chattanooga, Tennessee.